WAYLAND'S REVENGE

WAYLAND'S REVENGE

LESLEY LODGE

Matador
9 Priory Business Park,
Wistow Road, Kibworth Beauchamp,
Leicestershire. LE8 0RX
Tel: 0116 279 2299
Email: books@troubador.co.uk
Web: www.troubador.co.uk/matador
Twitter: @matadorbooks

ISBN 978 1789013 603

British Library Cataloguing in Publication Data.
A catalogue record for this book is available from the British Library.

Printed and bound in Great Britain by 4edge Limited
Typeset in 11pt Minion Pro by Troubador Publishing Ltd, Leicester, UK

Matador is an imprint of Troubador Publishing Ltd

Revenge is a kind of wild justice.

Francis Bacon

1.

1647, Forest Heath, England

With King Charles I now captured, the
Parliamentary forces are confident of victory

A man lay howling on the spikey stubble of a field. His arm was contorted. Blood streamed down his face. Three ravens strutted nearby, oblivious, slowing now and then to peck at the dry red earth. A young woman was walking slowly away, bent over in pain, towards a cottage beyond the field. A second man, Wayland, sat silent on the ground nearby. He too was wounded. The tattered strings of braid still hanging from their uniforms, the leather coats both men had cast aside would tell any observer that both men were – or had been – soldiers on the Parliamentary side. Both were injured and yet all conflict had ended since the King's capture.

Wayland heard the horsemen before he saw them, a good three fields away. At that distance, he couldn't tell much about them. He did know without doubt, though, that they would bring trouble. The only question was, which sort of trouble? Still he stayed seated, clenching and unclenching his fists while large bruises deepened in colour across his hands and face. The sound of hoof beats grew and grew. The ravens took off in leisurely flight, wings flapping slowly. Wayland remained in that exact position even as the cavalrymen surrounded him.

'What…' asked their commander, 'in God's name has been going on?'

The man on the ground spluttered. 'That… that bastard…' was all he managed to say before pain reduced him to a stifled groaning. Seconds passed. The commander dismounted. Seeing this, the man used his good arm to point at Wayland. The commander turned to Wayland. Now he saw the bruises.

'Have you not had enemy enough to fight without taking on each other?' he asked. Getting no reply, he threw his reins to the nearest cavalryman and strode over to Wayland.

Wayland stared back at him. 'There is still right and wrong,' he said, 'whether there's a war or no.'

'That's as maybe – but you? Justice is not for the likes of you to give. You are neither a commander nor a magistrate.'

'And neither a commander nor a magistrate was present here to stop a wrong." Wayland replied.

The man on the ground waved his good arm. 'Wait,' he said, 'wrong? I did nothing wrong.'

Wayland looked over in the direction the woman had walked but she was gone. 'If he did no wrong,' he said, 'then 'tis only because he was stopped.'

'Listen to me, both of you. In the absence of your own commander, I am taking command of this situation for now and I demand that you tell me what happened.' the commander said.

The man on the ground opened his mouth but thought better of it. Wayland said nothing. The horses fidgeted. The commander looked around. His men were looking bored too now. Then he saw the woman hobbling off, still just in sight. He grasped straightaway that Wayland must have taken exception to the other soldier raping – trying to rape – the woman. He turned to Wayland. 'So that's how it is. Well, *I* can inform *you* that injuring a fellow soldier,' he said, 'that *is* a charge. So I don't need you to tell me what happened. I can see him,' he a thumb towards the other man, 'and I can see that he's badly injured and you will have to answer to that.'

Wayland finally got to his feet. 'He'll live,' he said, looking at the man's arm, 'dislocation.'

'Dislocation? What do you mean?'

'His arm. Not broken. Just – in the wrong place,' said Wayland, 'and as it happens, I can help him.' He strode over and before anyone could stop him he had inserted both his hands into the right side of the man's coat.

'Breathe,' he said, 'breathe before I count to two. One... two.' He jerked the man's shoulder.

The man let out a scream that was pure animal. There was silence for a moment while all eyes were fixed on him.

His arm was no longer at an odd angle. He let out a low whimper and colour flooded back into his face.

'How?' began the commander, 'How did you do that?'

'Why, more like,' muttered one of the soldiers nearby to the fellow beside him, 'why bother to help the bastard?'

'Well,' said Wayland, 'as I say, there's more to life than this stupid war. A man's body doesn't work so very differently from a horse's. A blacksmith – that's me. That's my trade. Horses are my life.'

* * *

Later, back at his own regiment's encampment, despite a convincing outward calm, Wayland did begin to worry that he would likely face discipline. Army rules were set and he had, he knew, made matters worse with his continued refusal to explain his actions. Much as Wayland despised the man's treatment of a woman villager, he had, after all, succeeded in preventing her actual rape. Wayland considered the crime – if it merited such a label – already sufficiently paid for, in pain. And a common soldier's key to survival in these times relied on unwritten rules and these all reinforced the view that soldiers stuck together against officers.

The next morning, however, brought about a surprise change in Wayland's fortunes – or so it seemed at the time. Throughout the long months of his service in the war, there had been days of intense fear, days of defeat and days of victory. More often there had also been days of boredom. But there had never been a day like this one. What woke him early on this day was the sound of excited chatter.

'I can go then? Just leave, go home?' he heard a man ask.

'Aye,' someone replied, 'did you not listen? The King is captive, held fast for sure this time. They say Fairfax himself has him. Men like us, men who had no choice but to serve in this army, we are just another cost to them now.'

Wayland dressed quickly and joined the group of men outside. He stood at the back but he'd been spotted. 'Of course, that goes double for you, troublemaker,' said the last speaker. The other men turned to look at Wayland.

'Aye!' said one, 'I certainly wouldn't waste my time waiting if I were you. Which, thank the Lord, I am not.'

'Wait? Why would *anyone* wait if we can go now?' Wayland asked.

'The monies they promised us,' the soldier replied, with a smile that Wayland failed to notice, 'or are you so deep in trouble that money's no concern to you?'

'Nay,' Wayland said, 'but I'm not that naive. Have any of you been paid these last few months?'

Many shook their heads. All were silent now.

'So, if they didn't pay me my dues before, I see no cause to expect aught now, that's for sure. You can wait and hope for your pay. I'll be going now, back home. Unless they stop me.'

The news was spreading fast throughout the encampment now. 'Let's hope our women back home have followed a more faithful path than *some* men...' he heard someone say. This comment was aimed not at Wayland but at a couple of the men nearby. It raised a laugh. Wayland didn't laugh. He never doubted his own wife for one instant but still he felt a sudden chill of unease. He knew their village had not been touched by war. But he also knew that even in peaceful times life could be full of dangers, hazards – and evil men. Even more impatient now to leave and hoping no one else would be heading his way, Wayland hurried to stuff his few belongings into saddlebags. He reclaimed his old mare from the supplies and baggage section and set off home.

At first, as the mare picked her way slowly over the clods of earth cast up by cavalry horses, Wayland felt his mind empty of its day–to–day concerns. This moment had seemed an eternity away. Now that it had actually arrived, he could barely believe it. He was free to go home. Home to Rebecca, his wife. And to Jonathan, his son, who must be, what, eleven now? Back to his everyday life as a blacksmith. No more fighting, no more orders. Instead, he hoped, a calm existence to look forward to, though he did feel a twinge through his spine when he recalled the backache that went with his trade, blacksmithing.

His journey home took him across part of Suffolk before he reached Essex, his home county. From the outset he marvelled at the contrasts: while some places seemed untouched by the war, others were empty, more like ghosts' towns. He skirted the bigger towns, fearing some challenge as a deserter from those who might not have heard of the peace agreement, and slept in the fields at night. The word when he left the army was that Essex had been mostly saved from the chaos of battle, being safely on the Parliamentary side – the winning side, as it had turned out. He hadn't anticipated, though, the neglect that showed in the fields, the crops outgrown by weeds. Of course, he supposed, like himself, most men would have been called to war while harvest times had come and gone.

He was some five miles away from home, past Fyfield, when he began to recognise specific field structures for certain. Then his emotions broke through, twisting and churning as excitement mixed with apprehension. His senses seemed to sharpen. When he rounded the last corner into the road to the little hamlet where his home and smithy were, the very quietness reassured. Trouble would make a noise – wouldn't it? His heart jerked out a loud beat as he caught his first glimpse of the low, stone building that was his smithy. At first, everything looked in place. It took him a while to notice what was missing: the smoke. Of course, he thought, Rebecca wouldn't run the furnace while he was away. But then he realised, of course, there *should* be a fire going, for bread, for broth and so on. A small fire, yes, but you'd always see some smoke. He kicked his mare into a trot up to the door, tied her there and dashed in. He ran through the smithy, into the living area, barging at each door, shouting. No one answered. There was no one there. He yelled again, called her name. Nothing. Slowing to think, he checked the pantry. Flour was scattered across the floor. There was no other food. He thought again, and then checked for waste. Surely there would be food left, he thought, or rotten leavings, if… if Rebecca and Jonathan had been compelled to leave suddenly or – but he stopped himself, refusing to think through any alternatives.

It occurred to him then that he hadn't yet checked his animal pens at the back, behind the smithy. When he'd left, over a year ago, there'd been one old pig and half a dozen hens. The iron gate clanked and creaked as he opened it but he could swear he also heard a rustling. He could see no pig, no hens. Nor could he smell any animal. He pulled a stout stick out of the fencing and moved across the pen, thwacking the stick down on to the deep straw. He felt it hit a lump of something. There was a grunt of pain. A straw-covered something shot out and scrambled across the yard. It stopped at the fence and shook. As the straw fell away from the creature, Wayland recognised it. 'Jonathan!' he cried, 'Son! It's me, your father.'

Wayland scooped his son into his arms. He stood there, just stroking the boy's head as he would a nervous horse. But however much he soothed, however much he asked, he could not get the boy to speak a single word.

* * *

Wayland checked the smithy and its living areas once again then put the boy to bed. He set off, grim-faced, to find his wife. From the state of the boy he knew there would be bad news but he did not doubt that he would find an answer.

In the end, it took over three hours before he got any kind of an answer. Door after door, he found no one in – or at least, no one came to the door. Sometimes he thought he heard whisperings behind a door but no amount of pounding would bring anyone out to face him.

Desperate, he went to check the church. There, next to the church, at last a door did open. A very aged woman he knew only slightly stood looking out from her hovel. 'Ah, Blacksmith,' she said 'I always guessed I'd have you a-knocking one day. I suppose no-one else has the courage to tell you.'

'Tell me what? Where's my wife, Rebecca?' he asked, though her face told him she was dead, 'I have to know. What happened to her?'

'It was all lies of course, but there wasn't one who would say so,' she said.

'What? What was all lies? What happened? Don't give me riddles. Tell me outright.' Wayland wanted to take her by the shoulders and shake the answer out of her.

She looked around, fearful of being overheard. 'They killed her. Took her for a witch.'

Wayland heard a scream, a tormented, loud scream. It seemed a long way off. He didn't realize at first that it was his scream.

2.

One year later.

That year, summer was a long time coming and there were plenty in Essex who took the foul weather for a warning from above. There were unusual happenings, none of them good: calves born headless, owls falling stone dead from the sky and the like. Rumours abounded, too, of fresh battles between the King's men and Parliament's forces but that was way off to the south and people were weary of war. Wayland had been back home, working his smithy for so long now that his time in pressed service with the Parliamentary forces seemed a bad but distant dream. The discovery of his son half-starved, living wild and struck dumb and the fact of Rebecca's death remained a living nightmare though. Nevertheless, he stuck at his work, though business was slow with many of the village men still away, dead or nursing war wounds. His son, Jonathan, now twelve, was a small, crouched, smoky shape in a corner of the smithy, watching the sharp white sparks fly into the soft fleshy-red of the furnace. Neither spoke. The boy had still not spoken a word since his mother's death and Wayland seemed bent on hammering away something more than molten iron. Thirty part-formed pike points lay waiting. He still couldn't face working the finer stuff. He pounded on, absorbed.

Only when he rested the hammer a moment did he hear the disturbance outside. The smithy door opened, scraping across the floor. The sudden light threw a shaft of fizzing dust across the coke-dark smithy. Instantly, the boy scuttled soundlessly back into a corner. Two men crashed in, the brightness behind them casting their shadows huge across the stone floor. Wayland said nothing but he'd grabbed his hammer again. He flexed its haft now, pointedly, his arm muscles bulging. Both men stopped short. Wayland squinted at them through the light. These men were not built strong like Wayland; they'd grown up pale and spindly but as Wayland knew well, not all threats come from strength. The first man nodded to Wayland.

'Well?' Wayland asked, not lowering the hammer. Each man looked to the other to reply. Wayland realised then that he recognised them: Jack Whitman and Thomas Beale. Both were villagers, peasants once, labourers now, without fixed employment.

'Bring 'im in,' shouted Thomas Beale. A third man followed, dragging a horse. Head down, it shivered despite the furnace heat. Wayland recognised this man too: Thomas Beale's brother, Martin.

'We found a runaway horse. We want to know, can we keep him?' Martin asked.

'Keep him within the law and such,' his brother added for clarification.

Wayland stared at the men. 'You never give me the time of day these past weeks and now you come to me?' He knew, of course, that they came to him not because they wanted to but because in these times it generally fell to him to resolve all such matters to do with horses – and some matters to do with men – that didn't warrant the involvement of the magistrate, the magistrate being busy with problems thrown up by the lack of men around. Wayland didn't know for sure why most people shunned him of late but he knew for sure that things had changed since he went away. His strong suspicion was that the cause was shame, shame for something they'd done or not done. And that the shame was to do with Rebecca's death.

Wayland held his gaze steady in their direction until one by one all three cast down their eyes. Behind his father, the boy shifted very slightly in his corner, unnoticed except by Wayland. Then Jack Whitman moved forward, breaking the uneasy silence, scraping an iron bucket back over the stone threshold. 'Anyways, this horse needs water while you think on it,' he said.

Wayland moved quickly to block the man's path. 'Is that cold water, from the village well?' he asked.

The man nodded.

'You'll kill 'im with that. See, he's feverish. Never mind keep him – let's make sure he don't die.'

Wayland turned to focus on the horse. There was no head collar or bridle, just the coarse rope the men had used to steer him in. He noticed though some small cuts around its mouth, a telltale sign to Wayland of an over-used bit. There was no saddle either. He reached his hand out and the horse moved forward to nuzzle him. All three men drew back from Wayland – the old beliefs in blacksmiths' magic were not completely dead yet for all the efforts of the Puritans. Such superstition fed the villagers' reliance on him. The horse shuddered as Wayland ran his hand over its wet flanks.

'Saddle mark?' he asked. One of the men quickly scraped away the mud where a brand was likely. Wayland noticed then that the horse was not some uniform bay or chestnut but a rare dappled grey. His interest piqued, he appraised the horse more closely. Its slightly dished nose indicated breeding finer than that of the commonplace workhorse yet its general build was too slender for a soldier's mount.

'We did search round for his rider. But we reckon he's long gone. Don't he count as a straggler then? We want to keep 'un.' Again, it was Martin, the man with the bucket, who'd replied. Wayland caught a quick sideways glance between the Beale brothers. 'With your say-so,' Martin added.

Wayland dipped his hand into the water and traced his thumb over the horse's withers. He thought he could feel a lumpy pattern, but he said nothing. In theory, any final decision on keeping the horse would be down to the local magistrate but in practice – as these men knew – it was likely that as blacksmith Wayland was best placed to set about discovering the facts in this sort of matter and the magistrate, if later involved, would go along with Wayland's decision.

'Leave him with me,' he said. 'I'll make enquiries. Make sure if there's anyone to claim him. If not, well, we'll see. Give me a few days then.' He settled the nag in a spare stall.

The tallest man, Whitman, glanced at the others then nodded. One by one, they shuffled out. The door swung back into place, smothering the light again, leaving only the pink glow of the furnace and a grey square from the one sooty window. The boy crept out and poked the fire back to life. Wayland said nothing. Neither Wayland nor his son had been talkative by nature even before Rebecca's death and Wayland saw no point in trying to force it now. If the boy had not said a word about his mother's murder, he wasn't likely to start talking over a rider–less horse.

'Here,' he said, passing the boy a sizzling iron, 'take the edge off the water with this then fetch this horse some cut grass. Mind you fetch only the long stuff.'

The barest hint of a smile appeared on the boy's face and he set out, eager to tend the horse. After some minutes thinking through this new puzzle the men had given him, Wayland resumed hammering. His pounding had a more regular beat now.

* * *

In the past, Wayland would enjoy such small mysteries as these that the villagers would bring him. They stretched his mind, took him away from the repetition of his daily work. That was before though, before the war, before Rebecca's death and before his son had stopped talking.

Since then Wayland's thoughts so often turned to the revenge he'd take, so many kinds of revenge – if only he could find the man who'd killed her. Trouble was, these scenarios of vengeance would stop short, with a jolt, coming always to the same end: the reality that he was powerless and the only man he'd even heard mention of as maybe – only maybe –responsible was dead. Died of consumption some months after, is what they said. That much several villagers had told him, separately, but he did not always believe it. Truth was he did not want to believe it. They were, he thought, a little too keen to attribute the blame to a dead man. He had such a strong to hope it was untrue. For surely God must grant him some better revenge than a disease that took a man's life with barely a whimper let alone a howl of repentance.

Wayland's mood and some strong disinclination on the part of the villagers had hitherto kept most men and all the women away. Still, now they *had* come to him and within the hour he found to his own surprise that he was not displeased. He grudgingly admitted to himself that the mystery of the horse and its origins might intrigue him, lift his mood a little even.

So it was that only a couple of hours later he found himself riding out of the village, seeking not – as he would truly have wished – his wife's killer but some fallen rider. As his own bay mare picked her way past the narrow crop strips, he tried to fathom what sort of man might own such a valuable horse but fail to claim it. He'd have to be nursing some strong reason. Or maybe he was dead or wounded. Or perhaps it was fear: suppose he'd been thrown near the village but dare not face its inhabitants. All strangers were viewed with fear and hate in these days. Or was the owner guilty in some way perhaps? Wayland forced his mind to stop such speculations, lest he was imposing his own fantasies of revenge on the rider–less horse when surely there was more likely some simple explanation such as an accident. He pushed his thoughts in a different direction and began instead to wonder if the unknown man would be for Parliament, for King or for neither. Not that he cared too much one way or the other but these days it still paid to know which side a man favoured.

Wayland was at first easily able to trace the tracks made by the runaway horse, accompanied as they were by three sets of men's footprints, albeit they were jumbled sets. About two miles out from the village, though, the crops gave way to open common land. Here the earth was harder and the grass shorter. This area was dappled with a great many sheep droppings and there the men's footprints ceased. He decided to sweep the area, searching in a widening arc. Gradually, the grazed down earth gave way to scrubland and that in turn to young woodland. Noticing some broken branches, he urged the mare on through the gap until she took a sudden swerve, snorting heavily. He pulled her head back round until he saw what it was that had upset her. A raven had shot up from the shrubs and was still flapping violently. The mare reared up now in an uncharacteristic burst of energy. Wayland clung on, clumsily shifting his torso forward to avoid unbalancing his mount. He soothed her with a few quiet words and a stroke of her neck. Unlike many men, Wayland held no superstitious beliefs about ravens but he did dislike them for their stink of carrion and their habit of pecking the eyes out of newborn lambs. He looked around for any more birds for he knew they seldom travelled alone but he found no more. That was when he saw what looked like a pile of clothes, stuffed under a clump of twigs. He slid quickly off the horse, snapped a short stick from a nearby tree and used it to poke the top off the pile. Blood stained the clothes. The topmost clothes had a faint pink colouring to them. Deeper down into the pile, though, there was blood, a darker red, almost black. And it was wet and sticky. The clothes were small. They were the clothes of a youngish lad.

3.

ayland's heart began to pound while his calloused hands fumbled through the clothes. They had definitely belonged to a young boy. He didn't recognise them – but of course the war had taken him away for nigh on three years and most villagers had shunned not only him but also his boy since his return. He doubted he could recognise any of the village lads, let alone their clothes now. He called out and searched around but could find no sign of their owner. He thought about it: wouldn't a wounded child run home – if he could. There was no child to be found so perhaps the best thing to do was to return to the village, put the word around, check if anyone's child was missing. No-one had told him of any missing child – but then no-one had told him anything these months past, until his visitors today. The magistrate should know though. He rummaged through his jacket pouches, found some twine and parceled up the clothes to make a compact bundle he could tie to the saddle, behind him. He mounted up and put his horse into a brisk trot back to the village. He had to work at steering the mare on – she laid her ears back, reluctant, as they passed by his smithy and she expected her stable. At the magistrate's house he dismounted and thumped his fist on the door. Nothing. He knocked again, shouting out this time.

'Magistrate! I've important news! Open up!' He had to repeat this several times.

At last, there was the noise of bolts being drawn and the door opened. Stane, a runner for the magistrate, peered out. A smallish man, his already tight-skinned face stretched further into a sneer and his cheeks puffed out with self-importance.

'Yes?' he said, his tone seemingly chosen to convey weary indifference, 'What is it?'

But Wayland had already turned his back on him and was unfastening the clothes. 'Not you,' he said, without looking at Stane, 'the magistrate.'

'Well, then you're out of luck,' Stane replied, 'he's out of town.'

Wayland was generally slow to anger and his usually calm approach was key to his easy way with horses. What little tolerance or respect he had ever had for rank, though, or for those who assumed to rank had been greatly diminished during the war. He'd seen first-hand too many poor decisions made with such terrible consequences for those they commanded. He moved in closer to Stane. 'I reckon you'll have to do then,' he said firmly.

Although Wayland was not especially tall he was broad and with the angled sun behind him, his substantial shadow covered Stane, the doorway and part of the wall. Stane backed off. 'Say what you have to say then,' he said.

Wayland gave Stane a brief account of the runaway horse and how he'd found the clothes. He handed the parcel over. Stane picked it up, holding it out by his fingertips at the top of the pile, away from him. 'They're only peasant clothes,' he said, 'I doubt the Magistrate will be bothering himself with these. He's got better things to do. Have you not heard?'

'Heard what?' Wayland asked, despite a strong suspicion that it would be some scaremongering nonsense about the Royalists raising more rebellions or the like. It was.

'They say the King's men have left Maidstone. And that they're marching on London.'

'Last I heard, London's a good few miles from us here in Essex.' Wayland said. Wayland had fought on the Parliamentary side during the earlier civil war, had killed, wounded and been wounded, all in the name of Parliament. But that was under orders and if the truth were told he had little time for the moralising and self-justifications of either side.

'Fool,' Stane said, with a snort, 'd'you not see that if the King's men take London they'll likely win and all will be turned upside down again?'

'If this, if that... I've no time for it all. This, these blood stained clothes, may concern a child's safety. And that I do care about.'

Stane put the little pile aside on a shelf just inside the door. Grudgingly, he undertook to inform the magistrate on his return – and slammed the door.

Walking back through the village, leading his horse, Wayland felt a strong surge of frustration at this further unresolved issue. He decided to take matters into his own hands. He began knocking on each door he passed. Some houses were empty, their tenants off about their business, he supposed, or perhaps they were simply not minded to open the door. Of those who did answer he asked if they knew of any missing child. None did – or at least, none would admit it – and neither did Wayland's grim features and brusque manner do much to encourage any one of them to gossip or speculation. Disappointed, Wayland set off home.

Just as he reached the smithy, though, his son ran out across the cobbles to meet him, arms flying everywhere, tears on his face. He opened his mouth and Wayland felt his heart jump. Just for that second he thought the boy might speak. But no, he beckoned instead, urging Wayland on and scurried back into the smithy. Wayland broke into a run, tugging his mare behind him. He saw immediately that it was the runaway horse. Lying down in the stall it was shaking and sweating. It was moaning too, a high-pitched, continuous noise that had Wayland worried. He covered the horse up to its neck with an old blanket and piled some straw on top. Then he moved over to the forge and stoked up the furnace. Jonathan stayed with the horse, stroking its neck, while Wayland put a small pan of water on to boil. He scooped some of his own mealy oats from his cooking store, rustled through his herb bags until he found the herbs he was seeking. He took a handful from the bag but found he had to pause to think. His wife had been the real expert with such things. He ran the names of herbs through his mind. Rebecca would always recite some part of a long rhyme she had, to prompt her memory. Now most of that rhyme eluded him. He chose a mix of the most likely herbs, not too many lest they be the wrong choice. He stirred these in with the oats and hot water, making a warm mash. The horse was sweating now as he spooned the mixture into its mouth. Then, with a little of the left over hot water, he made the boy a light porridge. The boy refused to budge from the horse's side so Wayland brought the bowl over to him.

'Don't you worry, we'll get him through this, Jonathan, my son,' he soothed the boy, 'I've seen this sort of thing before.'

He put together a quick meaty broth for himself and began to stoke the furnace with the idea of using what was left of the day to tackle a small job he'd had for a while: making a set of cleaver-heads. He found he couldn't settle, though. His thoughts were whirling. He felt shortchanged by Stane. He could think of no explanation for what he'd found, other than some dreadful accident or maybe even a crime involving someone's son. He thought of his own fierce love for Jonathan and his heartbreak when he'd come back from service, so relieved that the war was done, only to find Rebecca gone and the boy struck dumb. He wanted this new mystery solved – and he wanted it done now. Later might be too late, he thought. He began to wonder whether with that much blood on the clothes their owner could be alive. He cursed himself for not staying to search round more thoroughly when he found the clothes.

It was now late afternoon – some hours of daylight remained. It was clear the boy would not leave the horse while it remained poorly. He laid the bellows aside, saddled up again and set off. Just at the edge of the scrubland some yards before the place where he'd found the clothes he hobbled the horse and left her browsing some green shoots. He kept an eye out for the raven or any of its mates as he searched again but none appeared. After a while, he found the patch where the clothes had lain. There were still rusty dots in the flattened grass. This time he looked more closely at the weeds and shrubs around, hoping for signs of trampling. Only after a long while did he find what he was looking for: some leaves and twigs flattened, others snapped. He bent down with some difficulty; blacksmithing had kept his arms strong, much stronger than other men's arms, but twenty years of bending and lifting had weakened his back. For the first time in many years he attempted to crawl. Hawthorns scraped his jerkin and his knees slid a little in the wet, black earth but he persisted. The trail was clearer at this lower level. He pushed on through the undergrowth.

He smelt it before he saw it. They say blood has a metallic smell but Wayland worked with metals and he knew the difference straightaway. Just to one side lay a contorted form, a small arm flung out towards him.

*J*t was near dusk when Wayland reached the magistrate's house the second time, cradling the small body to his chest. His knock, one-handed now, had less strength than earlier but this time, to Wayland's relief, the magistrate himself opened the heavy door. Wayland wondered briefly whether the magistrate had actually been away or whether Stane simply hadn't bothered to tell him Wayland was there last time. William Geddingly, a cloth merchant, had been appointed magistrate only last year as part of Cromwell's determined push to replace the king's chosen men wherever possible. Geddingly was a Puritan and took his responsibilities as magistrate most seriously – as indeed he did all responsibilities. Over the years his cares had etched deep worry lines into his rather long face and these now deepened further as he took in the sight of Wayland and his burden. From his house he dragged a small wooden bench onto the stone path outside so that they might examine the body outside in what light remained.

Between them, they laid the boy on his back and Wayland leaned in more closely. The boy's face was twisted as though still frozen in pain. The nose had been split open and dried flesh hung down onto his left cheek. He must have been about eleven, twelve at most. The hair, where it wasn't either bloodied or dirtied with mud and the like, was still reddish brown. With such wounds to the face it seemed impossible to figure out what he could have looked like before his injuries. Wayland studied the features and thought for a good few minutes. Despite the obvious difficulties barring any easy identification he was troubled by some hint of familiarity, of recognition maybe. But try as he may to recall any further, somehow all precision of thought evaded him. Not a relative, no. Maybe a playmate of Jonathan's from happier days. Some child his wife Rebecca had cared for and that Wayland might have seen, sitting at their hearth one winter, laughing and teasing with Jonathan, their own son. He was not at all sure though. So he said nothing.

The body was mostly unclothed but a bloodied under-tunic covered the chest. Wayland eased it up and they counted five stab wounds about the torso. The first was a lone, straight line and the next two were vertical slashes connected in the middle by a horizontal cut. The fifth wound, though, was a jagged swirl. Gently, Geddingly eased the small remaining cloth down a little, exposing the end of the swirl wound. The two men stood silent a moment, aghast.

'Any one of those wounds would have killed him through loss of blood – would it not?' Wayland asked at last. Geddingly stared at him.

'You don't agree?' Wayland asked, surprised.

'Do you not see?' Geddingly said, 'Can you not see? This one –' he pointed at the vertical slashes '– is a sign.'

'A sign?' Wayland looked closer, 'How do you make it that?'

'It's a cross.' Geddingly said, tracing the pattern in the air, his forefinger not touching but hovering rather, just above the boy's torso.

'But there are too many lines to it,' Wayland said, his face a blank.

'It's still a cross, a religious symbol.'

'Yeeess, I see you could make it that,' Wayland said slowly, 'so it's a Christian symbol then?'

'Yes. Of course. Have you learnt nothing in church? Nothing from the old teachings? Nothing from the new teachings? 'Tis a Papist symbol now, one we are now rightly to abhor. And Popery being the King's own religion whether he owns to it or no, this must surely hint at a Royalist killer – must it not?' Geddingly replied.

Wayland said nothing, not because he had no desire to be further mocked by the magistrate – though certainly he had not – but because he knew Geddingly to be fervently Puritan and therefore a firm supporter of Cromwell and the Parliamentary side, anti–Catholic and very likely seeing the Pope's hand everywhere. So he doubted that he'd secure an unbiased opinion. He gently wiped the edges of the boy's wounds and studied them again, hoping the appearance of such a cross was just an illusion the man had, influenced by his strong views. Yet in truth, as he wiped, he could see it more clearly now. The horror of the wounds alone had numbed his brain somewhat and he struggled to understand the import of Geddingly's discovery.

'Have you seen such signs before?' he asked.

Geddingly stared at Wayland, then looked quickly away. He didn't answer.

'What could it mean then? Does it signify some kind of devilish rite?' Wayland asked finally, more in puzzlement than in expectation of an answer.

'The Devil is in league with the Whore of Babylon so...' Geddingly began with an obviously well–practised rant about Popery but stopped short. 'But maybe it's more like a message, I would venture,' he said, more slowly.

'A message? But what is it saying? Does it tell us the murderer is a Papist? Or is it the murderer suggesting that this poor lad was a Papist?' Wayland's questions came quickly now, fuelled by his exasperation.

'There's little point in asking me. Ask a Papist,' said Geddingly, 'though it seems clear enough to me that no Puritan could do such a deed as this. I'd say it was some Catholic – and even then it would need to be a Catholic in clear league with the Devil.'

Wayland had his doubts that villains could be so easily separated from ordinary folk by the straight line of religion but he said nothing. They stood there a while in silence as the last light faded.

'Well,' said Geddingly at last, 'what to do? I'll get the body taken to the church for now. In the morning I'll start some enquiries. Coroner will want to hold some kind of proper enquiry but it'll be a couple of days before he can get here. Meantime, our priorities must be to find the boy's parents – and start hunting down his killer.'

'Very well,' replied Wayland, 'I'll be off now. You'll be wanting me for the enquiry?'

'Aye. You'll need to tell of the discovery. Farewell,' Geddingly said before pausing, 'but what about the horse? Stane said there was a horse.'

'Horse? Oh yes, the horse and missing rider. That'll have to do another day.'

'You see no connection then?' Geddingly asked.

Wayland thought a while. 'You may be right. Can't say that I see right off *what* connection though. No mere lad would have such a horse and his clothes don't speak to me of a wealthy father. And if it were the killer's horse, would he not have used it to get well away? Still, it does bear looking into.'

He wiped his hands down on his jerkin and set off back.

As he reached the smithy he stopped short. His living area – the part of the smithy building where he slept, cooked and sometimes washed – was in darkness already. He had expected that Jonathan would have lit a couple of candles on by now, maybe even have warmed some broth. Damn it, the boy was twelve. Yes he'd had a rough time, seen unknown horrors, had lost his tongue for over a year, but none of that should keep him from his duties. Or – he felt his heart start to thump – or something was not right. He walked up slowly to the door, holding his breath for quietness. Gently he turned the door handle. A little light from the rising moon behind him shone through the door.

Wayland saw the glint from the musket barrel first. There was a man, seated in Wayland's own chair, with a musket across his knee. The musket was pointed just to the right of the door.

5.

Naseby 1645, 14 June, a short way from the battlefield. About 2pm

*R*ees, a slight ten year old perched on an old, wheezing pony, squinted to focus through the whorls of smoke. He was worried. He had to get to the King's men's camp urgently, as soon as humanly possible, but he was lost. He'd been sent back and forth relaying the messages often enough to know that taking the wrong path would lose him a lot more time. He was starting to cry in frustration when, in the brief moment of calm after a volley of canon fire, he heard a clanging of pans. He knew then that he was finally near the camp. He kicked and urged the pony into a canter.

'Come on, old girl.' he urged the pony, adding a thwack from the rein ends. On arrival at the camp he reported straightaway to Elizabeth. She was married to one of Prince Rupert's foot soldiers and this tenuous link to royalty, plus the fact that she was both English and one of only a few married women among so many less obviously virtuous women, had given her some immediate status in the camp, at least during this time of war.

The message he relayed to Elizabeth was a fair, if shorter, version of what he'd been instructed to say. The King's men were outnumbered, as he'd said in previous reports. But that scoundrel, Fairfax, was proving more wily than expected in the way he'd mustered and moved his men. With God on the side of his anointed King, victory would still be granted – of course – but the women must prepare for more wounded; many more wounded. It could all be over sooner rather than later so they must make ready immediately. She thanked the boy and hurried to tell her friends. On foot, now leading the pony, the boy went across the camp to find his mother, Agnes.

Agnes Owen was already busy tearing sheets into strips, adding the strips to a small mountain of other makeshift bandages on the cart next to her and keeping at the same time an anxious eye on an open kettle of simmering herbs. She still sensed his approach though. 'Rees,' she cried, running over to him, 'what news?'

'Sshh,' he pulled her close, 'come away a moment.'

'I doubt anyone will hear us in this melee,' she murmured – but drew back quickly with him anyway.

They were far enough away and Elizabeth was in any case talking to one of the other English women now but he switched to Welsh, just in case.

'It's bad, really bad. None will say it of course but it's clear as can be. The King's men are losing – and losing fast.'

'Elizabeth's lot?' She meant the foot soldiers. Elizabeth's husband was a lieutenant with one of the key companies engaged in this battle. Agnes had formed a loose bond with Elizabeth and her husband – doing washing and the like for them – since Carter, Agnes's man, had deserted.

'Yes,' he said, his voice hoarse but urgent, 'but not just them, not just their company – the whole army, all of it. I mean it. I saw it with these eyes. They say it's on account of the hills – the rebel army's got the vantage. But it's not just that. Them rebels, roundheads, parlies, whatever you want to call 'em. They're no rabble. They're…' he paused, searching for the right term, 'it's like they're not individual men. They just all know, somehow, when to turn, where to aim – they do it all together. They're just unstoppable. And they're ripping our side to pieces.'

'But it's the King's army. The King, he has God – we have God – on our side. It's unthinkable that we would lose the whole battle. You can't be right.'

'I wish I was wrong.' he said – and with such finality that she knew it then.

'How many dead?' she asked.

'Too many to count even if I had time. Hundreds. I saw hundreds.'

'And the wounded?'

'Not so many but grave, really grave injuries. I saw so much blood on the field.'

Agnes turned to her pile of linen sheets. Her hands shaking, she resumed tearing strips. Rees grabbed her arm.

'The thing is… the thing is, our lot's backing off.'

'Retreating?' she asked, her voice pitched high in alarm.

'Sshh,' he said, tightening his grip on her, "tis treason to say. But they're coming this way, with the enemy close on them.'

In the silence that followed, Agnes turned to look over at Elizabeth and her group of English ladies. There was something furtive about their movements.

'Look,' said Agnes, 'I think the English women are packing up.'

'We should leave too,' said Rees, 'we must go – and now!'

'What? No. You know I can't. What about the orders? What about the wounded? Who'll bandage them? Besides, Fairfax's men won't touch us women. He's known for – how do they say it? – it's "chivalry" in English. They might take English ladies as good hostages but who would bother with a camp follower? Especially when they'll be wanting us to bandage their men too.'

Elizabeth and her maid were openly throwing valuables onto a cart now. Agnes looked at Rees again. 'Take the pony, quick, before she commandeers it,' she whispered, 'Parliamentary soldiers won't bother me – but you're a boy, a boy who'll make a man soon enough, God willing. You're an enemy to them. You must go – go now.'

'You're sure?' Rees asked, 'Should I not stay with you?'

'No. Get gone with you. Now!' she said, throwing her arms round him before pushing him away. Rees climbed back onto the pony, kicking it into a canter. He passed out of her sight, beyond the clearing – just as Elizabeth called out for a pony.

Agnes tore at the sheets, faster than ever, until she had a great pile of bandages. She had just turned her attention to pounding the now–tender herbs when she first heard the awful howling, a noise far more animal than human.

6.

Essex, 1648

ayland ripped open the door. In one lightning movement he leapt at the man, seized the musket from his hands and turned it on him.

'I see you've not lost your fighting instincts, then.' the man said calmly.

'Alun! You old sod, I could have killed you,' replied Wayland, dropping his raised arm, 'what on God's earth brings you here?'

Alun was Welsh. He was also a baker and he lived two villages away but he had some family connection with Wayland's local bakers and occasionally helped them out. Only twenty-eight, he looked forty at best. Years of breathing in flour dust had taken its toll and given him a wheezing cough that came and went in bouts. He and Wayland had been well known to take a drink or two together in the local alehouse, years back, back in the days before the war started up.

'I've heard you've been asking questions. Questions about a missing child?' he said now. There was an urgent edge to his voice.

'Bad news travels as fast as ever then,' said Wayland, 'but what do you know of it?'

'Our Rees, my sister's boy, has been missing these three years now,' Alun answered, his eyes searching over Wayland's face and finding an answer he didn't like.

Wayland said nothing. He thought a moment. That feeling of almost recognition that he'd had when looking at the boy's body. Could it have been Rees? 'How old would Rees be now?' he asked, stalling for time, dreading having to break the news.

'Thirteen I suppose, or even a bit more. I'd have to ask the wife. She keeps more track of that sort of thing and as I say, we've not seen him in years now,' said Alun.

'So... so could he have been as young as nine or ten back then, perhaps?' said Wayland, thinking back, 'when last I might have seen him, didn't he have blond curls and green eyes?' He hoped Alun would say yes. That should rule out Rees from being the corpse.

'Yes, blond when he was little. But his hair turned darker later. Brownish it went. Odd really but my wife says it's often the way with blond boys, turning darker. His eyes'll still be still green though.'

Wayland was silent, searching for words.

'Come on man, out with it.' said Alun.

'A boy's body been found –' he said, 'I doubt it could be him. If he's been missing three years, what would he be doing back here? I thought… I remembered Rees as blond though.'

'You *thought*? And now? You *think*…'

Wayland twisted his hands together, opened his mouth but shut it again.

'Lord, no!' Alun cried out. He slumped back into his seat. He struggled to compose himself but a deep sob wracked his chest and triggered a wheezing attack. Wayland laid the musket aside, leaned over and slapped Alun on the back until his wheezing ceased. Then he fetched a couple of jars and a jug of small beer. He filled one jar and passed it to Alun. Alun took it straightaway, drained it in one. Wayland poured another for Alun and one for himself. He sat down opposite Alun and began to tell how he'd found the body. He started with the rider–less horse and then the bloodied clothes. He stopped short as something occurred to him. 'Wait a moment,' he said, 'let's think this this through. If we don't find out otherwise, if no parents come forward for that poor boy, Coroner will likely want your sister to examine the body,' he said, then quickly added 'if only to rule out …'

'Well,' said Alun, interrupting, 'that'll be hard.'

'Why so?' Wayland asked.

'Well, our Rees didn't go missing alone.'

'No?' asked Wayland, puzzled now.

'No. My sister, she…'

Wayland nodded his encouragement.

'She ran off.'

'Ran off?' But even as he asked, Wayland started to remember there'd been some scandal around Alun's sister. Rebecca had been quite upset, hearing about it at the time. But of course the war – on English ground, between English forces, splitting families apart – had soon dominated all other news

'With some foot–soldier. In the king's army. Left David, her husband. Not that *he* was any loss. I never took to him. She took Rees with her, though.'

'We've difficult times now,' said Wayland, unsure really what else to say, 'and in difficult times people will do strange things, unwise things more often than not.'

'That's true enough, for sure,' said Alun, 'well, anyhow, he – David – took off soon after as well. I'm not sure I wholly blame him. Folks around made it clear they were set against him, whispers said he must have been at fault. You know how ignorant folk can be.'

Wayland knew well enough. He'd felt the pain of such attitudes himself. Alun continued, 'And, well, it became clear soon enough that she'd not be returning. He took it bad, though, about the boy, not knowing where he was...' Alun stopped short, suddenly aware again that in the light of Wayland's news, the boy's whereabouts might now be known. He spluttered, shoulders heaving. Wayland patted Alun on the back. Then, realizing that this was another coughing fit provoked by sobbing, he thrust the beer at him again. Alun gulped some down.

'The way I see it,' Wayland said slowly, 'if your sister ran off with a soldier from the King's army, they – and therefore the boy – must surely have travelled with his regiment. All the King's regiments have been moving a long way off. That must surely make it unlikely that your sister's boy could be, ahem, involved in this current discovery.' He thought it best not to mention Stane's recent scare–mongering on the subject of troop movements.

Alun looked up. 'Aye, I suppose you're right.'

'So, anyways,' said Wayland after a pause, 'as I say, one or the other parent needs to be found if no one else comes forward. Coroner will insist. Less you can claim relationship and confirm in public that the body is not his – or… or if it could be.'

Alun drew in a deep breath and wiped his face on his jerkin. 'So, carry on. Tell me about finding the body. Tell it from the beginning. And tell it straight.'

Wayland was silent. How could he even begin to tell Alun everything if there was still a chance it was his sister's lad?

'Well,' Alun said after a while, 'you could start with what's the connection then between the horse and the dead boy?'

'Good question,' said Wayland, 'and I don't know the answer. But I suspect it's a coincidence.'

'No,' said Alun, after a moment's reflection, 'it doesn't seem likely, does it, even in these strange times?'

'Let me… let me tell it all through – and we can talk about it when I've done.' Wayland said and he started to tell Alun about his first visit to the magistrate's house.

'Stane? That cocky bast….' Alun began – but he shut up when he saw Wayland's face and he let Wayland go on to describe his discovery of the body, his return visit to the magistrate and how they'd looked over the body together. He stopped short of mentioning the wounds.

'Such a young lad, so untimely. Who'd do a thing like that?' Wayland burst out.

'Wait up, man,' said Alun 'I thought we were talking of some accident. A fall from a horse or somesuch. Are you telling me it was murder?'

Wayland reached for his jar and took a long swig. Neither man heard the slight scuffling sound from the inner room. 'Murder and more than that,' Wayland said, his words coming out in a rush now, 'and the worst part was looking at that small body, the mutilations, the mess his killer made – and yet, somehow, the body so calm.'

'Mutilations? How do mean?'

'Just that. Not ordinary stabbings. There were signs gouged on his body. Some kind of cross–shaped signs.'

Alun was gasping for breath again, wheezing and sobbing. Wayland decided not to mention the slit that had disfigured the boy's face. There was a low creak as the inner door opened behind Alun. Wayland's son Jonathan walked in, slowly at first. All at once he flung himself at Wayland, sobbing and banging his head on Wayland's chest. Then he fainted.

7.

June 1947 Essex

onathan was really tired now. He'd been searching for his mother for some four hours. As he neared the next town, though, he heard a great noise, a kind of crowd roar. He stopped short and with a hurried knot, he tied the mare to the nearest tree and peered through the gorse bushes in front of him.

He saw five women, clustered together on a platform by a pond. Skirts flapped forlornly in the slight breeze and the boy realised the women's arms were tied. People swirled around the platform, some shouting, others laughing. Now and again, someone would lurch on to the platform, jab at a prisoner and a great yell would echo round the crowd.

Like most boys his age in those days, he had witnessed public punishments often enough before, of course, mostly *the stocks. He'd seen pain enough too and not just during the wartime. But here he could see no one in authority and that puzzled him. He joined the crowd at its edge, trying to blend in, unnoticed. He watched as the first prisoner was pulled roughly down and flung onto the mud. A knife flashed in the sun. Instinctively, the boy clenched his fists and sweat trickled through the short, fair hairs on his arms until he saw with some relief that the man was cutting twine, not flesh. Some men dragged a dirty, grey sheet towards the woman. He realised then two things: first that it was a swimming, a trial by water for witches. And secondly, that meant that it was not a punishment – as such – but a test: the innocent would sink, the guilty would float. That's what he'd heard. He strained to see better.*

Then he felt rooted into the muddy ground, powerless to look away. Conflicting thoughts swirled round his mind. He couldn't recognise anyone in the crowd. Young as he was, he could sense that some kind of mob fever had taken hold of them. It was drawing him in, too. He knew part of him wanted to leave but some other part of him had to look, to see it all.

Two men pulled up the woman's feet. Her skirts slid back and ribald laughter burst from the crowd. Roughly, the men tied her thumbs with twine, then her toes, then ran a line between the two bindings. There was a fumbling with the sheet as they wrapped her. Without meaning to, the boy started praying, out loud though he didn't realise it. Quick-fire, repetitive prayers. Lord, please stop this. Please God, help.

Three men waded into the pond, carrying their struggling bundle. As the water reached their shoulders, bubbles wheezed out of the billowing sheet. There was a shout. 'See: if you sup wi' the devil, you eat cabbage and fart!'

The coarse laughter spread through the crowd as the joke caught on. One man obligingly swatted the sheet again, provoking more bubbling. The men pushed her out, a struggling mass of cloth. For a moment her face was turned towards him, caught in a sudden streak of light from the sun. Then it was that the boy recognised her. Her desperate gasping reached his ears all too clearly. His prayers became incoherent now as slowly, so slowly, the bundle began to sink. Because that woman, the one covered in mud and being mauled about, was his mother, Rebecca.

8.

Essex, 1648

Wayland said nothing but picked up his son's slight form and splashed his face with a little of the beer until he came to and his sobbing started to subside. Wayland held the boy close and stroked his head, flattening the short hair, as he would soothe a horse. Gradually the weeping stopped and Wayland motioned for the boy to go through to the living area, to bed. He went. Alun, who had brought his own emotions under control, stepped back to allow Wayland a moment then shuffled his chair closer again. 'He do that often?' he asked.

'Happens,' said Wayland, 'from time to time. Since we lost Rebecca.'

'Lost Rebecca? Is there no end to our losses? Damn the accursed war.'

'Dead. Happened while I was away fighting in this – as you say – cursed war. I found the boy alone, living like some kind of hermit, scavenging food, venturing out of the house only at night. He's not said a word since. Me, I've said plenty. Reckon I went a bit mad at first. Shouted, yelled, swore at him. How could he not tell me what he saw? What I needed so much to know. For weeks I went from door to door, asking – begging eventually – for someone to tell me how come it happened.'

'And?' asked Alun.

'And I met with nothing but lies. From each and every soul I asked. No one saw anything – if you believe them all. Not a thing.' Wayland paused, topped up their jars. 'What I did discover was that some kind of witch trial took place...'

'That so-called General, Hopkins, was it?' interrupted Alun.

'That's the one. Called himself the Witchfinder General but that was no Government rank. Yes, him, some said. He was around, doing his accursed work in nearby villages, that much I did discover,' said Wayland, 'and of course he started the whole witch-hunt thing in our county from what I've heard. Found witches where there were none. But some said he wasn't the one to blame. And – well, I've also heard he's dead anyway...'

'And good riddance,' Alun butted in, keen to keep Wayland talking now that he'd begun to open up.

'Yes. Well, I'll come to that. Anyhow, this... this supposed trial, they tell me it was more like a mob, a rabble. There's no proof that this Hopkins led this trial. No papers were shown; no person claimed any authority except that of God. And any man can claim that, it's easy enough. Seems they tried five women, including Rebecca. Three had been dragged here from the next village so of course I went there too, looking for answers. No one there would talk to me either. The fourth was old Mistress Bland and she had no relatives left alive – so I drew a blank there too.'

'How ended the trial?'

'Two were judged guilty. None came out alive though,' said Wayland.

'It must be at least four years since I saw her,' Alun said, 'but Rebecca a witch? She was no witch and there's no way that I can see why anyone might even think so.'

'No, well the hell of these wars, families ripping themselves apart, turns minds, no effective justice, confusion over who does hold the power when it changes so. Clearly it was no Royalist thing, not at all. Hounding witches comes from the Puritans. And though they're thick in with the Parliamentary lot, well, I had a year in their army. Cromwell's men are better organized than most and Fairfax – I'd rate him the best of Parliament's commanders. Fairfax would be their man around here, in Essex, at that time, if anyone was. I know him to be a man who keeps a tight rein on his men, a lid on their basest instincts so to speak and he is well recognised for it. But as I say, from what I've heard this was no army thing neither but a mob. And I've seen enough to know that men can – and generally do – change nature in a mob. They just don't think right – or straight.'

Wayland paused, staring into his beer. Alun waited.

'What cuts me to the quick is,' Wayland continued, 'is: where were our villagers in this? Did no one testify for

45

her? Were they all rank cowards – or worse?' Wayland slammed his beer jar hard on the table. The liquid sloshed onto his breeches but he took no notice.

'Weren't most men likely away, like yourself?' asked Alun.

'Aye. I suppose. But what about the lads? The women, then? All I got was sideways looks and silence. Alun, I loved Rebecca. If there was someone still alive, if I just had someone to hold responsible – or one who helped in any part of it, I'd have my revenge, so help me God I would!'

He paused. 'Some days I think about nothing else,' he added.

Neither man spoke for a while. Wayland shifted his weight on the wooden stool and rubbed his spine. His return from war back to the smithy and to work had, as he'd feared, brought with it the old back pains from bending over the furnace or horses' hooves. 'So, Rebecca – she was found innocent but drowned, then, was it?' Alun asked.

'Yes. Well, I suppose so. Pulled alive from the water but died anyway. That's all I know.' Wayland turned his back on Alun. His shoulders shook. Alun waited another moment.

'This man Hopkins. Dead for sure, then, you say?' he persisted.

'Consumption, I heard. And I heard it time and again.' Wayland turned around again and Alun saw that his face was white with rage. 'He's gone. The way I see it, whether he killed her or no – he did start this… this obsession for finding witches everywhere. That I do know. I would have made him pay. Oh, how I would have – or died in the process. His death has cheated me of my revenge. It stays, the vengeance, locked in my heart, devouring me slowly in my innards.'

There was a long silence this time. They both sipped some more.

'At least you have your boy. Maybe, maybe you should think more on that,' said Alun.

Wayland was silent. He knew Alun had no children and now it seemed possible his nephew was dead. Alun drew a deep breath before continuing, 'there's nothing wrong with your boy's tongue, is there?'

'No,' Wayland said, 'not anything that I nor anyone can see.'

'Likely his speech will come back then, one day. Meanwhile, remember that revenge belongs to the Lord. Maybe you should leave it to him, look to your boy.'

'Easily said. But understand this: that revenge is in my blood. Or... or it's like a thirst. I *cannot* leave it alone. The only way I see to cool this anger is to make justice be done. But as you well know, with the country torn apart there's little law left untouched by one side of the other.'

Both men drank some more. 'About your sister's boy Rees, then,' said Wayland, finally, 'where would be the places to look for either parent?'

'I don't know. It's such a long while now since she ran off and left us. We tried then. I doubt we'll find out now. And all for some foot soldier in the King's army...'

Wayland interrupted him quickly. 'You'd best ask around then. If the father's to be found, magistrate will want to see him.' he said, reaching for the musket and passing it over to Alun, handle first.

'I suppose so,' said Alun, doubtful, 'but it might be easier to start looking for the bastard she ran off with. My wife will likely remember his name and regiment. Then maybe I should check in the alehouses.'

There seemed nothing more to say. After a moment Alun picked up his hat. 'Right. Well, I'll either send word or maybe see you tomorrow then?'

Wayland nodded and opened the door for him. He watched Alun step into the road before he began to heave closed the wooden door.

Alun turned. 'Just a thought,' he said, 'the wounds on the boy's body. Would they relate to religion? God knows religion has caused enough violence these past few years.'

Wayland paused long enough that he appeared to think about it. 'We might look into that,' he managed to say. But Alun had gone.

9.

The next day passed with no further news and Wayland struggled to control his impatience, telling himself the apparent return to a sort of normality should be welcomed. The day after, though, Stane showed up at the smithy, early in the morning, with a message from the magistrate summoning him 'and whomsoever you believe may know any further facts concerning the recently discovered body of a boy' to attend the coroner's inquiry that afternoon. Wayland got ready, leaving the door to the smithy barred and gave Jonathan instructions not to open it to anyone. He rode straightaway to fetch Alun. As he feared, Alun had made no progress in his attempts to find his sister, his brother-in-law or the soldier who had lured his sister away. He did agree immediately, however, to accompany Wayland to the inquiry.

The few villagers in attendance at the little hall by the church moved aside without a word to let Wayland and Alun pass. A group of men, already selected by the coroner for the inquiry, stood at the front. The boy's body lay on a table, covered by a grey cloth. Wayland was grateful for the unseasonably cold weather but still the stench betrayed the likelihood that corruption and decay of the body were indeed under way. The coroner gave a brief explanation of the facts, as he understood them to be, of the discovery of the boy's body. Wayland was asked if he had any further information. He replied that he had not. The coroner stated that in his view the cause of death was clearly the wounds on the body with a loss of blood and – or – the consequent shock and damage to the vital organs. He added that the body seemed almost drained of blood and that in his view might account for the relatively slow decay of the body. He asked the chosen men to step forward and examine the body. They filed by, each man with a cloth pressed close to his nose. One of the men – they were all known to Wayland – had obviously been chosen to act as spokesman and he reported that they were all in agreement with the coroner's remarks.

The coroner then announced his verdict: murder with gross cruelty by person or persons unknown. Wayland realised that there had been no mention of any possible religious element to the wounds. He thought that by now decay may have blurred the lines and he reflected that neither the coroner nor the men chosen for the inquiry were likely overly knowledgeable of religious matters or symbols. The coroner cleared his throat and signaled his clerk to be ready to write. 'It remains only, now, to attempt to determine the boy's identity and to set in train some way to bring the guilty to justice.' he announced.

Alun stepped forward and asked permission to see the body in case he may be able to identify it as his missing nephew. The coroner agreed and raised the cover from the body for him. Alun stared at the small form. He shook his head.

'No?' asked the coroner.

Alun shook his head again.

'No it's not him?' the coroner asked a little more loudly.

'No, no I don't know,' Alun replied, 'it's too… I can't tell. I can't say.'

The coroner turned to the men beside him. 'Show him the clothes.' he said.

Alun picked at the bundle, tested the cloth between his finger and thumb and shook his head again. 'I don't know,' he said, 'it's years since I saw him. I just don't know.'

'Well, if you cannot say, can you at least suggest who could?' The coroner was waiting; the clerk's hand hovered over the coroner's large record book. Alun, however, could only stand, open-mouthed, rooted to the spot. Wayland stepped forward and explained the matter of the missing sister to the coroner.

'This,' said the coroner, 'is not satisfactory. Even in these difficult times we must at the very least record if the corpse is from this place or a stranger to this place. If, as it seems, no-one knows for certain then I must record for now what steps are to be taken to establish such facts.'

There was a short silence. Magistrate Geddingly stepped forward. 'Might I suggest,' he said, 'that as we have no other men available or –' here he pointed to Alun 'or it seems at least none capable – I say we appoint Wayland here, who found the body, to find the boy's relatives – if it can be done.'

The coroner looked around, directing his gaze to each man in turn. Some shuffled, most looked away. No other suggestions were forthcoming. 'Very well,' he said, 'then so be it.' Wayland knew that he was being offered little choice in the matter, but he could also see that Alun was in no state to respond. He nodded his acceptance to the magistrate. The clerk duly entered the decision into the record book. The coroner thought a while. 'And,' he said, looking at Geddingley, 'I am also minded to direct that the task of enquiries shall be aimed at discovering the killer – if that can be done.'

Geddingley opened his mouth. He seemed about to say something but thought the better of it. The coroner then ordered the body to be buried and declared that the inquiry was done. Men began to drift away, their mood subdued.

Wayland took Alun's arm and led him away. He paused for a moment outside then tightened his grip and steered them both towards the alehouse nearby. It was one thing to accept such a mission. Now they had to work out how to set about it.

10.

ayland was standing beside a lake, watching thick grey clouds swirl over the seething water. At first he could hear only the waves slopping against the shoreline. Then a woman's head broke through the surface of the lake, gasping, choking, panting. Wayland leapt forward, ran towards her, shouted to her to hold on, to wait for him. But her head sank down again. He could see only the black surging sea and some dirty white foam.

His own cries woke him, but it took him a few moments to realise he was in bed, in the living area of his own smithy, sweat trickling through the hairs on his body. He shook off the damp covers, walked through to his stove and poked the fire back to life. He went to check on the boy, Jonathan, but found him still asleep, curled into a foetal position. The boy was used enough now to the regular disturbances of his father's nightmares, so they seldom woke him. Deciding not to rouse him yet, Wayland went through into the stabling area and began mucking out his horse and the runaway horse. Both were standing, with faces pressed to the iron bars. Wayland was pleased to see that the runaway seemed to have made a full recovery. He checked him over thoroughly anyway.

He'd just laid the clean straw down when Jonathan joined him. Wayland handed him a bucket and indicated that he should feed the new horse. The boy half-smiled, went up to the horse and blew down his own nose gently to the horse's nostrils – the initial greeting a horse will give another horse. It gave Wayland some pleasure to note that his son was picking up a blacksmith's ways. He said nothing, though, and father and son fed and watered the two horses together, prepared a basic breakfast of bread and small beer for themselves and ate, all in a companionable silence.

Wayland went through into the smithy and stared at his tools. Business had changed a great deal since the onset of the civil war. There was much less shoeing work since the army had taken most horses away to war. The demand for repairs or new weapons – pike tips and such–like – tended to come in fits and starts as various army units came by the village, on their way to or from rumoured trouble spots. Often there would be no payment for these and because of this Wayland had taken to hiding his raw iron so as to strengthen his bargaining position. There was nothing waiting for him to do in the smithy that was either urgent or even likely to bring in any income any time soon. He went back into the stable and checked the runaway's feet more thoroughly. They were sound, dark hooves. All four still had reasonable wear left in the iron shoes but he hammered a couple of new nails into the front ones just to be sure, ready for any eventuality.

He and Alun had talked long into this last night; that is, Alun had talked and Wayland had made the occasional point. All they had agreed on so far, though, was that Alun would check with his wife and her brother for any possible leads to the whereabouts of his sister, her husband or her lover. Wayland reflected now on how it was that he found himself thinking all the time about the poor boy's body. He felt a little guilt for his neglect of Rebecca's death. He asked himself again and again what sort of man could kill and so mutilate a young lad. In times like these, communities – families even – were split. People died, people killed each other. It wasn't uncommon. But usually they did it in the heat of battle or at least as part of the war. They didn't carve religious or other symbols on to bodies afterwards. At least, he didn't think they did. So what did it mean? It must mean something else why do it? Geddingly had said the gashes formed a religious symbol and Alun had also suggested that there might be a religious element to the crime. Might it be some reference to the country's bitter religious divisions? And if so, to which side did it point the blame?

Wayland thought hard on this angle. Who could – and might agree to – tell him more? Catholic priests were long gone from this part of Essex and he couldn't think that any Puritan would be open-minded enough to give an unbiased answer. Then a thought came to him: he remembered an older, wise woman that Rebecca, his wife, used to consult occasionally on questions of herb medicine. She lived a little way out of the village and seldom ventured back into it these past few years, deeming it too risky since the mania for finding witches had sown suspicion even into the minds of ordinary people. He decided to visit her.

He told Jonathan he'd be out for a good while, saddled his horse and set off. A brisk wind and scudding purple clouds promised yet more rain and it was still unseasonably cold for summer. He wasn't too sure of the way – Mary had been Rebecca's acquaintance not his – but a number of landmarks such as the end of the animal enclosures, the old gibbet on the hill and the abandoned mill did look reassuringly familiar as he passed them and after about half an hour's ride he found himself outside Mary's ramshackle hovel. Still mounted, he called out her name a few times. Nothing. It occurred to him that perhaps his voice was a bit deep, intimidating, maybe, even to a wise woman. He notched it up an octave and tried again. Then he slid down, tied the mare to a sapling and strode up towards entrance. He noticed just before he got there that the door had been smashed and was lying to one side. The two chairs and the table inside had been upended and a number of cooking pots lay scattered on the mud floor. There was no sign of any inhabitant and, at first, he decided the place must have been abandoned.

He moved towards the doorframe, noticing some crude scratching on it. He traced them with his fingers. They were numerous circles, each overlapping. Next to them was a more structured etching of one circle with two smaller circles, each of a slightly smaller size.

Within the smallest circle was some kind of formalized petal pattern. Below all of these the letters "AM" had been roughly carved. 'Mary!' he called again, trying for an even more friendly tone. He sniffed the air. There was a faint odour of cooking: cabbage and wild bird maybe. So much for what *was* there. He tried to focus on what was not present and he supposed there would surely have been some scent of mould or at least mustiness if the place had been without occupants for any substantial length of time. His senses tensed again and he felt his neck hairs lift. He had the distinct feeling that he was being watched. He turned around to face the door. Mary was standing there, a thin, dark figure, silent, just outside.

She looked even older than he remembered and he doubted whether she had washed or changed her clothes in a long while. 'Mary,' he said, attempting to smile in what he hoped was a reassuring way.

'Ah,' she said, "tis Rebecca's husband, is it not?'

'Yes. Wayland, the blacksmith. But Mary! What happened here?'

'It's nothing, really,' she said, coming into the house, 'they've turned the place over so many times I leave it like this. Then they don't bother again.'

'They?' Wayland asked, 'who are they? Men seeking witches?' He pointed to the crude markings on the doorframe.

'Aye,' she said, 'they hope to rid themselves of me by marking my home for a witch's house.' She pointed to the lettering in the wood. 'I tried to speak back to them in their way. But they wouldn't have it. AM is for Ave Maria, of course. But it serves too for Auld Mary.' she added, a slight smile forming on her face.

'Mary!' Wayland reproached her, shocked at such casual blasphemy.

'They call themselves God–Fearers, Puritans and the like. I call 'em rabble,' Mary said, 'but let's not worry about them. What is it you want? Is it to do with Rebecca?'

Wayland thought at first that she may not have heard about Rebecca's death. He told her the basic facts – such as he had discovered. Mary said nothing, but she righted the chairs, sat on one of them and gestured to Wayland to take the other. As he reached the end of his account, Mary covered her face with her hands and let out a low moan. She rocked gently back and forward. Wayland reached a hand towards her, but she flinched. He drew it back. 'Aye, I did hear.' was all she said.

There was an awkward silence. 'But, well, it's another death I've come about.' he began, unsure how to start.

'Not her son, Jonathan?' she asked quickly.

Wayland winced at the words *her son*. 'No, thank the Lord, not our Jonathan. But a lad not much younger.'

'Who, then?'

Wayland told her briefly how he'd found the boy's body.

'That's sad, I know,' Mary said, 'but alas, it's not so rare for these cruel times.'

'True enough, I know,' Wayland said, 'but as to the times, firstly, there's been no fighting round here these months past. And secondly, as I say, the lad was only young – he looked no more than ten or eleven. And thirdly – and this is the reason I've come to you – thirdly, there are strange wounds on his body. Mutilations, really, they are – but in a pattern. Some kind of religious symbol I've been told. And I wondered if you might be able to tell me anything about them. Something that might help point to the man – or men – who murdered the poor boy.'

'Religious you say?' There was more than a hint of bitterness in her voice, 'Would that be the new God-fearing religion? Or the old religion?'

'I don't know, Mary,' Wayland said, running his fingers through his hair. He was afraid that to say one or the other might disincline her to help. 'I simply don't know. Maybe religion even older than that.'

'Heathen? God forbid,' Mary crossed herself – once a simple enough Christian action but now one outlawed in Puritan eyes.

'No, not heathen. At least, I don't think so, from what I've been told. Here,' said Wayland, 'I'll show you.' He fetched a strong twig from outside and crouched down on to the mud floor. He drew on it – as best as he could – the pattern of the wounds he'd seen on the boy's body, the unusual cross and the slashed face. 'These,' he said, pointing to the long straight slashes, 'these I reckon were the death wounds. But these,' here he pointed to the lines across, 'when the magistrate saw these, he reckoned that together they make a cross. Some kind of special cross, I guess.'

Mary appeared to think a while. 'The Cross of the Crossed Keys. That's a Christian symbol all right and widely known as such. I doubt that tells you much though. It's not disputed; you'll see it in church, even today,' she said. She moved closer, looking down at

Wayland's rough sketch. 'But I suppose such a cross could be considered a Papist symbol now, more likely than not. If you've drawn it as it was,' she continued, more confident now, 'then, yes, it's clear to me. 'Tis the Crossed Keys indeed.'

'Crossed *Keys*? These loops would signify the keys' handles then?'

'Yes.'

'But keys to what? A money chest? Is it a message about money?'

'No, not that,' Mary said, impatient now, 'did you learn nothing in church – the old church I mean?'

'Tell me, just tell me,' he said, trying to hide his annoyance, for although he had quite deliberately withheld from her what the magistrate had already said, he nevertheless found he disliked being thought ignorant, even if it was only ignorance of church matters.

'They're the keys to heaven.'

'Ah, right.' he said, trying to sound as though he followed her explanation.

'It's a Crossed Keys cross,' she said slowly, 'so it represents the very keys to Heaven, as given by God to St Peter. And St Peter's powers, it used to be said – '

'Were transferred directly to the Pope, that bit I do know. So, all right, I see the way that goes now,' he paused, 'but the face markings,' he moved the twig up to the top of his crude drawing, 'would they be religious too?'

'The face markings, now they're a different matter.' she said, crouching closer to look more closely at Wayland's sketch.

'Yes,' said Wayland, 'that's what I was thinking.'

Mary frowned. 'Draw the face again,' she said, 'and draw it separately and bigger, here. Just show it as it was.'

Wayland gripped the stick in concentration, struggling to remember the detail of the boy's pale body, upturned by the magistrate to maximize the fading light. He drew the face again on the dirt floor, larger this time, with its slit across the nose, the flesh hanging down. He carried on, sparing no detail of the mutilations that he could recall. He heard her sharp intake of breath. He looked up at Mary, waiting. He saw something change in her face. 'What?' he asked, 'what is it that you see?'

Mary looked away, not answering at first. 'Well, one thing is: it's what I don't see:' she said finally, pointing back at the drawing of the torso, 'you've drawn more details now. But how could a man carve such intricacies on the boy's soft body? There'd be blood, mess, the lines would blur.'

Wayland was quick with his answer. He'd seen enough corpses, days after battle, when men – scavenging, careless and rough in their haste – cut into dead flesh. 'No,' he said, 'not if the carving was done some time after death.'

They were both silent a moment, thinking through the implications of this – and united in not liking them. A murderer who mutilated the corpse seemed somehow much worse than one who slashed in the heat of some moment. 'Anyways,' Wayland said, 'going back to what it all means. If it any of it means aught. Do you think it a message of some kind then?'

'It may be, yes,' said Mary, 'though nowadays the crossed keys are a symbol used only by the old religion. Catholics. Or Papists as some now would say. Think on the teachings from church. God gave the keys to heaven to St

Peter. St Peter's representative here on earth is, of course, the Pope. So, a meaning might be to stress the pope's authority and –'

'And by extension the authority of the King then, as upholder of the pope's authority.' said Wayland quickly.

'So maybe the killer is for the King.' Mary said.

'That would figure,'

"Or, if not the killer, then at least the brute who carved the sign.'

They thought about that for a moment.

'No,' said Wayland, running his hand across his eyes, 'no, the killer must be the one who did the carving. He has to be. I can't believe – I *won't* believe there could be two separate men out there wanting to inflict such horrors on an innocent lad.'

Mary looked away. 'I would wish it were true,' she said, 'but all my years have taught me there's no limit to what evils men can and do think up.'

Saddened, Wayland pulled himself up from his crouched position on the floor and rubbed his aching back. 'I thank you for your time,' he said. He had decided to leave but it troubled him that Mary had avoided his question about the boy's face. 'The nose, then,' he said, 'do you see a further message there?'

Mary looked away again.

'Tell me,' he insisted, 'you must say. I can see you think something of it.'

'I cannot tell you what it means, exactly,' said Mary, 'but I can tell you where it's from. And then maybe you'll understand what kind of message it might be. Whoever did this has a history. And bloody one too.'

'Tell me then. Tell me.' Wayland pointed to his dirt floor sketch. 'The slashed nose. What's that about?'

'A sign. It signified ... a whore.' she said at last.

'A whore? Not a witch?' Wayland asked.

'A whore: a woman who has lost all virtue, at least in the eyes of some. It's nothing to do with witches or wizards or the like. Not that such poor souls who've had the slash were generally either witches or whores.'

Wayland was silent. He'd told Mary – and more than that, he knew he'd told himself – that he'd come here because of the boy. But he knew too that his thoughts were never very far from Rebecca's death. Everything always came back to her: plants, herbs, cats, his son and now a body. It was stupid, a long stretch, to think there'd be a link; but he knew he was condemned, like some tragic hero from an old legend, forever to look for one. If he had found a witchcraft connection in the motivation perhaps there would have been some lead, however tenuous, to what happened to Rebecca. He knew now that he was just clutching at straws in the wind. Still, he asked himself, didn't the boy's death deserve an answer too? 'But then why this lad?' Wayland thumped the floor with such force that a gritty dust enveloped them, 'What could he have had to do with it?'

'The slashed nose,' she said slowly, 'you see, that's from Naseby.'

'Naseby? Wasn't that a battle, oh, some three years back when Parliament routed the King's men? If it is the same one, then I don't follow.'

'Not the battle itself. I'm talking about the massacre after.'

'Massacre? What massacre? I've not heard of one.'

'No,' said Mary, 'it's not one that either side cares to talk about. It was a massacre of women, you see. News spread fast enough amongst women, from one side of the country to another even if men thought nothing of it.'

'Women, then? Was it only women killed?'

'Camp followers,' she said, watching Wayland's face closely.

'You mean, ah, the soldiers' mistresses and the like?' he asked.

'I mean womenfolk,' Mary said – there was an edge to her voice, '*just* womenfolk. Who d'you think bandages the wounded, patches them up, after a battle?'

'Women, then,' said Wayland, 'but what happened?'

'Welsh women these were. And I know you fought on Parliament's side, so you'll not want to hear this.'

'You know it's true that I did fight for them,' said Wayland curtly, ''tis also true that I had no choice in that. It was that side that pressed me. It is that side that controls our part of the country.'

He paused, guilty that perhaps he had overstated his views. 'Though it's also true,' he added, 'that I would pick Parliament against the King each time if I had the liberty to choose for myself. But then again, it's true that in what they call the heat of battle, in my view, there's precious little to choose between one army and another. Men – even men who've had no calling to fight, who had no choice but to join – they can – and often do – fall into some kind of blood lust. Things happen in war. So tell me now, what happened?'

This speech, such a long one for Wayland, surprised them both.

'Things happen, yes,' said Mary, 'but this was a matter of hundreds of women, slaughtered after the battle. Cut down and cut up.'

'Cut up?'

'Slashed and run through, mostly. But here's my point. Their killers – and they were Fairfax's men, fair and square, no getting away from it – they marked every single woman they caught, dead or alive, with a slit to the nose. Just such a mark as the likeness you have drawn here shows.'

'But why?' Wayland asked, with such force that saliva sprayed from his mouth, 'Why?'

'They split the noses,' Mary said, 'slit the whole nose, right from bottom to top, as a lasting sign to others, so that anyone and everyone would know these women to be whores. That's what was said. But to my thinking, it was more likely to justify their own evil actions, to persuade people there was some purpose to it. There was some talk too that they mistook those Welsh women for Irish women, as if that justifies it. If you ask me, though, in that moment, it was just that they hated all womankind, pure and simple.'

They were both quiet a long while. 'I can – just about – follow that,' said Wayland, 'though I'm not – not at all, you must understand – not at all saying that I condone it. But what I must return to, is why the boy?'

'Perhaps,' said Mary in a slow voice, 'could it be, perhaps, that it was about the boy's mother?' Her words sent a shock snaking through Wayland's chest and his mind filled with images of knives slashing his own wife, his own son. In a haze, he gave Mary a brief farewell. She did not reply though, and he went towards his horse.

He was about to mount when a thought struck him. 'Wait,' he said, 'there's something you're not saying. Mary, what is it?'

'They say,' she said, 'though I don't know the truth of it – they say that Rebecca was slashed something like that. I'd not thought of a meaning, though, until you drew those marks.'

Wayland couldn't speak, couldn't think. He just left.

11.

Wayland kicked on his horse so as to cover the ground more quickly on his way back. His visit to Mary had resulted in more information but yet, at the same time, he felt more pain, confusion and frustration than when he'd set off. He could think of nothing he could do with the information other than, he supposed, report it back to the magistrate. He knew though that if he ever caught up with the killer – would it be one killer? – anger would explode in him. Rebecca. The boy. Just a young boy. In what world could that ever be justified?

When he called at the magistrate's house, he saw with some satisfaction, that Stane was a little less arrogant on opening the door and went away without a word to fetch the magistrate. Wayland told Geddingly what he'd heard about the slashed face wounds and their possible symbolism. It was only right that the magistrate should have all relevant facts if, as directed by the coroner, he was to look into the matter. He told him briefly that he had explored some possible explanations of the patterns in the dead boy's wounds 'with one well versed in such things,' he said, being careful to keep Mary's name out of it. He knew that as a traditional 'wise woman' she – and certainly her remedies – would be regarded with deep suspicion by many men in these times but most especially so by a puritan such as the magistrate.

'Lord knows the Papists and their allies get up to evil deeds and murdering children is an evil deed for certain. As all know who care to know, the King is a Catholic in his heart, whatever he claims in public. So I'm inclined to think it does indeed look like this points to a King's man as suspect,' said Geddingly, 'but as my man has – I understand – told you already, the King's men look to be coming this way. They're closing in even now. And as the magistrate, I am the only authority Parliament has here right now. What can I, one man, do against an army? The King's men would be in no mood to hear about this. Even to mention aught about it could set off violence. My first duty is to ensure order is kept here as far as possible while our villages suffer the King's men's stay, if indeed they come. And for the sake of our villages I will not want to give them any cause to stay an hour longer than they need.'

Wayland thought a while. 'Well,' he said, 'I suppose I can see that. But as I think, there is naught, is there, to hold back the boy's uncle from asking around? I'm talking about the Welsh baker as he is the man who may be that poor lad's only relative.'

Geddingly picked at some piece of fluff on his coat, unconvinced.

'I'm remembering the coroner's words,' Wayland said, 'he said someone needed to, ah, make enquiries. So, if not the baker, how about myself? Since, of course, you know me to be a sober man, one who has paid his dues and fought for our side?'

'Don't *you* be telling me of my responsibilities. And don't ask for my approval. The less I have to do with this the better.' Even as he said this Geddingly flushed, shamefaced. 'At this moment.' he added.

Geddingly moved towards the door. Wayland moved faster so that he was between him and the door. He then stood there, blocking it, fixing him with a stare until finally Geddingly looked him in the eye.

'Go then if you must. Come back, though, when the King's men have gone,' he said, dropping his voice, 'let me know what you find out – if you find out anything.'

Wayland knew that this was as close as he would get to an instruction to investigate further. He stepped back to let the magistrate pass and the man was straightaway gone, retreated back into the house. Before Wayland could call out his thanks or farewell, though, Stane popped his small round face out, gave a malicious smirk and snatched the heavy door shut.

Alun's house was only a little out of Wayland's way home. He decided to call in, to let him know what he'd reported to the magistrate. As he turned the corner into the little street for Alun's house his horse nearly trod on a small girl who was poking sticks down the rat holes that inevitably surrounded any bakery. Alun himself came out when he heard Wayland and the girl talking. 'Good day,' he said, wiping his floury hands on his apron, 'come on in. I owe you a jar.'

'Or two,' said Wayland, seeing that Alun's mood was much improved. He tethered the horse. 'Besides,' he said, 'I've some progress to report.'

Alun looked up, expectant.

'Nay, I've not found the killer. Nor even your delinquent brother in law.'

They went in and over the first jar of ale Wayland gave Alun a short account of what he'd been told and what he'd reported to the magistrate. Again, he kept Mary's name out of it, even though he knew he would trust Alun a great deal further than he would the magistrate. Alun listened in silence. 'So we're not much further forward really, are we?' he said after Wayland had finished.

'No,' said Wayland, 'but we do have leave – of sorts – to look further into this.'

'But I've news too,' said Alun, 'do you remember what I was saying before, about our Agnes?'

'She ran off with a soldier some years back?'

'That's right. Shamed us all. Ran off with one of Prince Rupert's foot soldiers.' He spat onto the mud floor.

'Have you found her then?' Wayland asked.

'No. But I have heard word that the bastard she ran off with has been seen, spotted in this county. Alone.'

'Alone? That's … not good, I suppose.'

'Seems to me he must've left her, and God knows where she is or how she is now. Carter his name is. He was a nasty type anyhow – as I told you, I never trusted him. Beat his horse for a start. And there was just something about him.'

Wayland nodded in agreement. In his trade he had seen many horses made ill, infected through spur or whip cuts inflicted by their owners. Most men did it because they didn't know better, because they simply wanted to make a horse do something the horse didn't want to do or was just plain too scared to do. Every now and again, though, he'd come across someone who actually enjoyed hurting the animal. He had found that such men were always – with no exception – unpleasant and cruel in their dealings with women and family too.

'I'm planning to seek him out, to find out about Agnes – and the boy,' Alun said and then added, 'I could use some company – would you be in for that? We'd probably be away three days or more.'

Wayland thought a while. He was pleased that Alun had recovered somewhat but he doubted that it was likely a full recovery. As regards to himself, well, business was slack, and without Rebecca the smithy – nay, the whole village – was bleak to him. His recent contact with Alun was pretty much the only protracted human contact he'd had in a long while other than the silent company of his son. Plus, he was feeling a real need to delve further into the matter of whether Alun's nephew might be the dead boy. The murder was so wrong that something must be done about it and it didn't look as though anyone else was likely to take it up. Besides, looking into things had been part of his life, an interest that relieved the tedium of daily life. Until the matter of the runaway horse and the missing rider it had been a long while since he'd been asked to investigate or advise on anything.

'Where in this county?' he said, at last, 'Where is it that have you heard he is?'

'Somewhere north of Witham is what I heard. Drinking himself stupid no doubt. If – as seems likely – he is no longer with the army then we have some chance to find him still there, I reckon.'

'Witham. That's a fair ride out,' said Wayland, 'and if we're away a several nights or more, as you say, then I'd have to take the boy.'

'You do? Is he not of an age to be left?'

'In normal times, yes,' said Wayland, 'but these are not normal times. In the state he's in, not talking and that, and after what happened before when I was away, I'll not be leaving him behind. I suppose we could settle him somewhere in town, when we get there.'

'So you're in?' Alun thumped the table, bringing up a cloud of flour, 'We'll sort ourselves out and set off tomorrow, shall we?'

'I suppose so.' said Wayland. He stood to leave.

'Bring something from the smithy, then.' said Alun, winking.

'Something?'

'Something heavy, like – something you can use as a weapon.'

'It's to be like that is it?' said Wayland, 'Didn't you just say you wanted to find out about Agnes? You've not got some kind of revenge planned?'

'I think the man who's obsessed with revenge is you, not me,' said Alun, 'and anyhow I doubt we'll need to get rough if he's the drunkard I think he is. But it's best to be prepared. So… bring something.'

12.

ayland was on his way back home, just reaching the outskirts of his village, when his eye caught a small movement, by the animal enclosures. The far one was empty, save for some crows picking over the droppings, but just beyond them he saw a man crouched over the well, his arms working at the chain. Wayland could just make out a flat–ended, coned hat fixed to the chain in place of a bucket. The man sucked up water greedily. Wayland nudged the horse over towards him.

'Hello there, stranger. Who might you be and what is your business?' Wayland called out.

'Don't hurt me, sir,' the words were intoned dully; the man's eyes downcast, as if he had no energy left for fear.

'Have you lost your horse?' Wayland asked, riding over to the man.

'Horse… I've been walking. Ah, have you food, please sir?'

'Have you money?'

'I have the Lord and he shall provide. Maybe you are his instrument, sir?'

A door slammed somewhere in the distance and immediately the man crouched down, his face finally alive.

'Don't let them find me. Look – look, what they did.' He pulled up his jerkin and then the ruffs of his tattered sleeves. The flesh beneath was torn and infected.

'Who did that? The army?' Wayland asked, knowing full well that neither of the two armies would thank him for helping an enemy.

'No, Sir, not the army. Neither of them. Nor the Justice either. Let me tell you later. I must get away.'

Wayland hesitated. If neither military was responsible, he reasoned, it was probably men from the villages. Most of the law–abiding ones were still signed up to one army or the other – or dead. Wayland had experienced first hand the hostility of those left behind, even before they'd turned on Rebecca. And he knew what it felt like to be an outsider; he had long thought of himself as an outsider. Blacksmiths were not gentry of course, but they were not as poor as most other folk either. So his instinct gave him some sympathy for this man. He hoisted the man up and laid him over the horse, explaining his hope was that, from a distance, his load might pass for firewood.

Back at the smithy, Wayland saw immediately that Jonathan was out, but he said nothing to his guest. He led him straight through to the living area and set out what food he had: some rye bread and a little herbed oat porridge. He saw that despite an obvious hunger, the man ate in a mannerly way.

'Are you a godly man then?' his guest asked, looking at Wayland's meagre belongings.

Wayland considered a moment. These days a man's place on the spectrum of religious fervour could, and often did, cost him dear. 'We are all godly men now. Aren't we?' he said. He searched the man's face for signs of either enthusiasm or scepticism, but what he saw was defiance.

'What's your name?' Wayland asked.

The man hesitated, looking quickly around. 'Erasmus,' he said finally, 'Erasmus Fynche'

'Wayland, blacksmith of this parish some twenty years.' Wayland replied. He waited, but there was no rejoinder. 'Well, what's your story?'

Silence. Wayland looked directly at the man but found it uncomfortable. Part of the left ear was missing and he tried, out of common courtesy, not to focus on it.

'What am I to do with you?' Wayland burst out at last, 'The law has it that I should report all newcomers to the Magistrate, whether they be visiting relatives or felons.'

'I am a simple man, passing through, with no friends in this place,' the man said, 'and I find that the men here are uncouth."

Wayland stared at him, trying to hide a growing repulsion for the man and his whiny yet pompous composure. He took him through the stabling area. Wayland's horse snickered, happy at first to see Wayland. But the other horse laid its ears back flat on to its head and backed away when it saw Erasmus.

'Well. Sir, are you sure you do not know this horse? A man who knows horses might assume that this horse knows you,' Wayland said, "even though you told me you had no horse.'

'Yes, yes, all right, that's my horse,' the man said, 'the brute threw me.'

'What startled him?'

'Nothing startled him. He's simply evil. Evil through and through.'

'I've never met an evil horse,' Wayland said, 'there's generally some reason for bad behaviour.'

'Let's not talk of it, though I suppose I must thank you for finding him.' Erasmus replied.

'Don't thank me,' Wayland said, 'a couple of men from the village found him.'

'It is somewhat dark now,' said Erasmus, 'might I trouble your hospitality a little more?'

'You may stay the night, if that's what you want,' Wayland said, 'but no more than that. I've only animal bedding to offer but 'tis clean.'

'Thank you, blacksmith Wayland'

There was a silence then and Wayland decided that anyway he was in no mind for further talk either. Instead, he pointed Erasmus to the long–deserted pig stall next to the smithy and gestured for him to bed down on the straw.

Later, Wayland heard his son come back in and go through to the stable. He guessed he'd be fussing over the new horse. He listened a while, remembering his guest's description of the animal as evil but he heard only the sound of gentle patting. Wayland sat a while by the stove, supping a small beer before calling the boy in. Wayland realised that just as Erasmus was ignorant of the boy's existence, so too was the boy unaware of Erasmus. He decided, though, not to mention their visitor. He reasoned with himself that it would only upset Jonathan to think that they'd be losing the horse. He realised also, though, that he was somehow uneasy about Erasmus. He double-barred the door. When he finished his ale, he called the boy and together, without further words, they went into the sleeping area adjoining the smithy.

It was a long time, though, before sleep came for Wayland. His mind conjured, as it did most nights, over and over, his revenge on those who killed Rebecca. He saw himself ask each faceless man after another that appeared to him, why? Why Rebecca? Someone had told him once the parish paid out handsomely to witch-finders. forty shillings a witch, they'd said. That was more even than Cromwell's foot soldiers got for two months' hard slog. What had been Rebecca's price? Who received the money? Who paid it out? But again, and most of all, why? These thoughts gave way, after a while, to nearly as many questions about the dead boy but eventually he did fall into a restless sleep.

Next morning, Wayland started laying out his implements in the smithy. His guest, he assumed, was still asleep in the pig stall. There was a sudden loud pounding on the door. Wayland just managed to kick shut the inner door, blocking off access to the sleeping area and the back of the smithy, before Stane, the magistrate's runner, burst in. Again, his face was distorted by that self-important sneer.

'The Parish is looking for a fugitive,' he said, 'a man on the run.'

'And?' asked Wayland, allowing his disinclination to help to be obvious.

'And I thought perhaps you'd seen him.' Stane's tone made it not so much a question as an accusation.

'What's this one wanted for? Murder? Thieving?' asked Wayland.

'No,' said Stane, only a little deflated and embarrassed, 'it's, well, it's that he's not from round here. That's serious enough, in these times, is it not?'

'These are difficult times, I'll agree. The war has left many folk on the move. But must we suspect all of them to be wrong-doers?'

Stane didn't answer immediately but it was clear that he was about to. Wayland decided he didn't care what weasel words Stane would come out with. So he spoke again to forestall him. 'So now, how come you let this one get away?'

'*We* didn't. There was no signing from the magistrate for this one in the first place. From what I hear tell, it was the townsfolk, they caught him, they held him – and then they turned to us when he got away.'

Wayland tried, he really tried, not to say what came straight into his mind. But he failed.

'So it was a man then, not some poor woman this time?' Wayland struggled to keep his voice steady while inwardly he fought an urge to hit Stane. If Stane did realise that Wayland's cryptic remark was only just holding back a dammed-up, huge reservoir of Wayland's emotions he gave no sign of it.

'Happen there's all sorts of miscreants and witches. Still, no matter, they all end the same. The rope gets 'em if the water don't.'

'And proof?' Wayland asked sharply.

'We always get a full confession.' Stane smirked, 'Two or three sometimes.'

Wayland knew full well that Stane had powerful connections. So he understood the risks and likely consequences of upsetting him, but he went straight up to Stane regardless. He thrust him out and slammed the door.

Wayland stood a long time in thought. 'Fugitive,' he muttered to himself, 'townsfolk.' Finally, he opened the door to the horse stalls. The runaway horse was standing there, calm and untied. He checked the other stalls, then the living area. He went into the old pig stall. He looked outside. Nowhere was there any sign of his visitor – and nowhere was there any indication whatsoever as to which way he'd gone.

'I guess he heard all that,' Wayland said quietly, to himself, 'well, one less problem for me to worry about.' He turned to the horse. 'And maybe one less problem for you too, my boy,' he said to it, stroking its neck just underneath the long wavy black mane.

13.

That day passed with no further sign of Erasmus. Stane looked in briefly again but soon left, without a word, apparently satisfied no fugitives were being harboured there. Wayland woke early next morning and checked round once more for Erasmus. As he suspected, there was no sign of him. The horse was still there. He woke the boy and told him they were going to Witham.

'We may be away a couple of nights or more,' he said, 'so bring what you need, but not too much, mind.'

Wayland packed his own essentials in an old leather sack that doubled as a saddlebag. As always, he also loaded a basic kit of tools from the smithy. It was not that he was minded to follow Alun's admonition to take a weapon. Taking the tools of his trade simply made sense to him. There was always the risk that one or other of their horses might cast a shoe and there was also the possibility of earning something along the way if a stranger's horse needed a few nails or his cart required fixing. He remembered Stane's earlier words about the King's men being on the move and he thought too about the likelihood of more general trouble. He found one of Rebecca's old herb lists and wrote down on the back of it a brief testament to his ownership of each of the blacksmith's tools that he'd packed. As an afterthought, he added to the list a description of the two horses – their colouring and brand marks. Both horses had unusual brand marks, though not, it was true, the same brand and the runaway's brand was barely discernible. With only a slight qualm about claiming the runaway horse as his, he signed his claim to ownership with the number and the rank he'd had when serving in Parliamentary army those three long years previously. He stuffed the list into the pouch on his mare's saddle, beneath a dirty cloth.

Next Wayland cast his expert eye over the runaway horse and ran his hand down each of its legs. The horse seemed fully recovered now, with no lingering signs of fever. Usually, if he had to take Jonathan anywhere with him his son rode pillion, but this was becoming less comfortable for both of them as the boy grew. Besides, he reasoned to himself, he could hardly leave the runaway horse to fend for itself indoors. True, he'd be risking the villagers' ire if they found out he'd taken the horse but, after all, he'd be bringing it back. He found an old bridle that fitted. He had no spare saddle so instead he threw a sheepskin pad on to its back and fastened it under the belly with a leather strap. He led both horses outside.

Jonathan ran straight up to his mount and stroked its head softly, down towards the whiskery hairs and dark pinkish skin of its nose. The horse snickered and Jonathan smiled his thanks to Wayland. It seemed to Wayland that in that moment his son looked so very different, his whole face taking part in the smile. He tried to remember when Jonathan had last smiled – but he couldn't. When that realisation hit him he was shocked: it must have been some long time before. Before Rebecca died.

When they turned into Alun's road, they found him already packed up and mounted, ready and waiting. 'Did you remember? Did you bring...' Alun began, but he stopped short, seeing Jonathan, 'I mean, did you bring everything?'

Wayland said nothing, but he nodded in a general way. The three of them rode on together. Reaching Witham on their second day, they found it to be a quiet town with no sign of Carter or soldiers of either side. Alun suggested they enquire of the local baker and so they did, stocking up first on some bread patties. The baker directed them on towards Brantry. He said he'd heard of forces passing that way, though he was cautious in describing them. The little party set off again. They were perhaps some four miles out from Brantry when they passed eight or nine men walking briskly. Alun greeted them with a cheerful 'Good–day!' but not one of them returned his greeting. He turned to Wayland. 'Cousins of yours?' he asked.

'No,' said Wayland, surprised at the question.

'Only they're almost as talkative as you...' Alun said solemnly.

Alun thought he saw a hint of a smile cross Jonathan's face but Wayland scowled and said nothing. Alun kicked his horse on until he was parallel with Jonathan.

'Hey, you're not exactly a fine conversationalist either, are you?' he said. A pink flush rippled over Jonathan's face and he looked away to fiddle with the sheepskin pad.

The passing men were soon followed by more men, then by a couple of family groups. At first Alun continued to give his cheery "Good–day!" but not one of them gave him any answer back. 'Odd.' said Alun, to no one in particular.

They heard the excited chatter of the next group before they saw them. About twenty young men swaggered by, laughing and play–fighting. 'Good–day young sirs,' Alun began again.

A couple of them turned their heads to look behind them.

'Fool,' said a third to the first two, 'he's talking to us.'

'Could you tell us, please,' continued Alun, 'where everyone's off to and why so gravely?'

The youths paused, looking to one another for support. 'We may as well, if we speak carefully.' This was from the third youth again. He seemed to be their unspoken choice for leader. He turned to Alun. 'There's a, ah, commotion in the town. The King's force has arrived…' He left the sentence hanging in the air.

'In some haste, you might say,' added one of the others.

'Which force would that be?' Wayland asked.

'It's not so easy to tell for sure, as it happens, with the chaos there is and so on, but Sir Charles Lucas is there, and most men seem to answer to him. Our town is mostly for

Parliament, so we thought it – as you might say – a good choice to leave for a while.'

Wayland nodded, Alun thanked them and they passed by. 'The magistrate did tell me the King's men were coming,' Wayland said, once they were out of earshot, 'but I took no notice at the time. Maybe we should turn back.'

'Turn back?' said Alun, 'And miss out on finding Carter? Rather, I think, we should crack on, find him before Lucas's men find him.'

'Why should it matter if they find him? He's one of them, is he not?'

'Think on it man,' Alun said, 'if Carter's alone – as I heard he was – why would you think he is?'

'Ah, I see. You think he deserted.'

'Yes. Either this last week or so in Kent. Or maybe sometime before. Maybe after some other defeat for his side. I don't actually care what *his* story is except that I want to know where my sister is and what *her* story is.'

Wayland said nothing.

'Look,' said Alun, 'I know it can't be the same as how you feel about Rebecca. Agnes is my sister not my wife. She's likely brought about her own ruin. But we've heard nothing. She may be all right. Or she may be dead. And more than all that, there is the matter of the boy. You of all people should know well how all that feels – it's the not knowing. Such not knowing has eaten away at you this whole year past. This thing is starting to eat away at me. Point is, we need to get to Carter before Lucas does.'

Wayland kicked his horse on ahead and the three of them carried on into the next town. The first stalls they passed were deserted but boarded up. Further into the centre, though, there they did find, as the young men had said, a great commotion. They saw some of the King's men, all disheveled, some partially in uniform, some stripped down to breeches and tunic, all of them beating with weapons or even fists on doors or hauling away food and drink. Wayland stopped only to drape their cloaks over their bulging saddlebags. 'If we're asked,' he hissed to Jonathan, 'if anyone questions you, we're on a mission, sent by Prince Rupert.'

'But a mission for what?' Alun asked, 'And anyway, *he's* not likely to say anything to anyone, is he – if he doesn't speak?'

Wayland glared at him. 'Arms,' he said, 'repairing weapons; we've smithy duties to carry out.'

'I look like a smith?' Alun asked, 'I mean, do I?' With his frail frame hunched over the saddle, he had a point. But they rode on. They passed several groups of soldiers without challenge. Wayland spotted an alehouse. 'Carter likes a drink, you say?' he asked Alun.

'Carter likes drink *a lot*,' Alun replied, 'or certainly did when I knew him. Drinkers seldom change.'

They roped the horses to the posts provided across from the alehouse, choosing the shady end, not for its protection from any sun – yet again there was none – but because it afforded some cover from any rain and from any curious eyes. There had not been one day without rain in eight weeks and they certainly did not wish for questions from nosy locals. Wayland pushed open the heavy inn door. Immediately the acrid smell of sweat and beer hit them. Wayland walked straight to the serving hatch with a firm tread and without turning his head. His eyes, though, quickly took in the scene inside. There seemed to be two groups in the room. The first set of men appeared relatively sober. They were seated around a couple of tables, speaking in low tones. Further away there were men propping each other up or loosely clutching at the supporting posts. Several had passed out altogether, slumped across the tables or lying on the floor amid a mess of wilted straw and herbs, pools of spilt beer and upturned tankards. The landlady, her face red–veined and sweating, trotted out an automatic "good day" to Wayland and looked about to enquire into the origins and destinations of the three new arrivals. Before she could ask, though, Wayland spoke. 'A good day to you also, madam. Two tankards please of your finer beer.'

Something tugged at Wayland's jacket from behind. He jerked round and seized hold of something. It was a hand.

14.

Naseby. 1645, 14 June, Afternoon

*T*he howling became louder, nearer. Agnes could make out individual screams now. For a moment she felt paralysed, rooted on to the earth, her hands still holding the strips of cloth. Then she dropped the cloth and she ran, holding her skirts up out of the mud. Other women soon overtook her; their urgency spurred her on. Tree branches whipped at her face and caught at her skirts. Neither she nor any of the other women wasted any breath screaming now. All that Agnes could hear was the sound of her own lungs heaving and that of her heart drumming. She lost a shoe, sucked into the wet clay. Its loss made her lopsided, unbalanced. She kicked off the other one and ran on. She began to hear hideous noises – thudding and groaning – behind her now and she realised with horror that the faster women were out of sight, ahead somewhere. Or were they behind? She risked a glance behind and glimpsed a melee of what looked like clothes on the ground – dirty, moving clothes. She saw men in red and grey – soldiers of the other army, the King's enemies – jabbing at the clothes with pikes and swords. She knew in an instant then that the jumble of clothes must actually be a group of women, the King's army camp followers, women like herself. She could hear them now, screaming in Welsh and in English.

Agnes thought quickly. She knew that just ahead must be the road that led eventually to Leicester. There would be no hiding place on such an open road. So she ducked sideways and thrust her body through the hedge. Hawthorn scratched her face and ripped at her chest but she barely noticed. She stumbled over the lumpy earth, searching, praying for a hiding place. She heard a loud grunting and cursing – and then the rasping sound of a hedge being forced as a soldier burst through. She thought quickly and turned to face her pursuer. 'Stop!' she shouted, 'Are these your orders? Does your general order this?'

'Irish!' the soldier said, 'I knew it.'

Agnes was puzzled for an instant until she realised that in her panic she must have spoken in Welsh. 'No!' she said firmly in English, 'We are not Irish. I am not Irish.'

The man hesitated. He made as if to lower his sword, but a second man crashed through the hedge, quickly followed by three more. 'Hey, John,' he said to the tallest man, 'this one says she's not Irish.'

'I am not Irish.' Agnes repeated, loudly and clearly.

'Well, if she's not part of that murdering tribe, then what is she?' the man called John asked, moving closer to stare at her. A short, older man, his face disfigured by a leering scowl, pushed his way to the front. 'I'll tell you what she is. She's a whore just like the rest of them.' he said. Agnes saw that he was holding a small dagger.

He darted forward and grabbed her hair. All of Agnes's senses seemed heightened. In the few seconds it took she could smell his vile breath, see the thick spittle moving around his mouth and feel his fingers hooking through her hair, his nails tearing her scalp. He stared direct into her eyes. 'Beg,' he said, 'beg me for mercy.'

Agnes begged. In short, repetitive gasps she begged. He forced her onto her knees and laughed. 'Nehemiah,' she heard one of the other men say but it seemed to her that he must be far away, too far away, 'Nehemiah...'

Agnes felt a jolt of pain and then the hot blood running down her face as the dagger slashed up through her nose. 'That's how we mark whores. So all men will know them and their dirty ways. But it's not enough, not with these whores.' he hissed.

Even as she felt so much fear, knowing he meant to kill her, Agnes felt time slow down. She seemed to notice every detail. She noticed that part of his ear was missing. She saw his breeches rising with an erection. There was screaming all around now and two women partly stripped naked, their bodies cut by the spiky hedge, surged through the hedge. Agnes saw their faces, too, were bloodied and one was bleeding around her neck. Soldiers followed, more and more of them. They were all shouting but the words were incomprehensible to her now. The first woman tripped and immediately a group of men swarmed over her. An arm held up a lump of flesh.

Agnes's mind was working fast. It recognised the men's bloodlust for what it was. It knew about the deadly momentum of a frenzied mob. But search as it might it found no way out for her. Her attacker twisted her face around, lowered his dagger from her face and slashed it into her chest and downwards.

15.

A village outside of Brantry, 1648

Jonathan ducked away from his father's fist just in time and pulled back, looking at Wayland in surprise.

Wayland adjusted his stance quickly, converting his aggressive thrust into some kind of clumsy head pat. 'Ah, and, ah, one tankard of small beer.' he said to the landlady. She nodded and poured their drinks without a word, being careful, now that she'd noted the speed of Wayland's reaction, to fill them to the top. Wayland led them to the one unoccupied table and they sat a while, drinking their beers. 'See him here?' Wayland asked of Alun.

'No, but…' said Alun.

'But what?'

'Well, there's no-one in uniform that looks like him, that's clear,' said Alun, 'but I suppose… I mean, it's possible, he might have discarded the uniform.'

'Aye, for sure – if he's deserted.' said Wayland.

A small, scrawny man on the next table looked round at them as if straining to hear them. 'Sshh,' Alun hissed, 'do you want one of *them* looking for him, to seize him and collect the reward for a deserter? Finding him and handing him over, gone before *we* get to ask him questions?' Then, more loudly, he said 'Yes, I'll have another – if you're still paying.'

Wayland, his face blank at first, caught on at last. 'Paying?' he said, just as loudly, 'As I recall 'tis your turn, fair and square.' The scrawny man went back to his original conversation with his companions. 'Here,' Wayland said to Jonathan, 'take this money and buy us some food.'

Jonathan didn't move. His face looked a silent question.

'Nothing fancy. Bread of course. Maybe some barley broth if she does it.'

The boy still stood there. 'Ah. Yes. Well, just point and nod then.' Wayland said.

'And smile,' added Alun, 'smile as you point. It helps.'

As soon as Jonathan set off to find the serving girl in the kitchen, Wayland grabbed Alun by the elbow and led him to the far end of the room. He pulled up the first drunk's head by the hair, turning the man's face towards Alun.

'Hey, Smithy, what the…' asked Alun.

'This one,' Wayland interrupted, 'is this him?'

'No,' Alun said firmly, 'it's not – and I don't think…'

Wayland laid the head back down, none too gently. Alun watched the man's eyes drift shut again.

Emboldened, he followed Wayland to the next prone form and the next and the one after. None of them was Carter. As they moved back towards Jonathan and their seat, though, Alun spotted another body, crumpled up in the far corner of the room, behind a large sleeping dog. This man's mouth was open, distorting his face, but Alun felt a flicker of recognition. This time he was the one to pull the man's head up.

'Wayland,' he called, 'I think this one's him.'

Wayland strode over. 'You're sure?' he asked.

'Not really,' said Alun, 'not sure. But I do think it.'

Wayland pulled this man up by his sleeves. Alun nodded to Wayland and went round to stand the other side of him and between them they hoisted him up and took him over to their table. Alun staggered under the weight but Wayland bore his share easily. They propped him up on their bench and made a show of sitting with him to finish their ale. 'Here, old boy,' Alun said loud enough for the other drinkers to hear, 'I think you've had enough, that's for sure. We'll get you away, you can come back with us now.'

They pulled the man up again and set off towards the door. One or two of the other customers glanced up as they made their way slowly out but not one made a move to stop or question them. Jonathan ran out after them, clutching some lumps of bread and they soon reached the horses. Round a corner, away from the horse stand, was a stone trough. Wayland perched their load on the edge of its nearside wall. He used the leather bucket that was chained to the trough to scoop up some of the greenish water from the trough and poured it over Carter's head.

He waited while the man choked, spluttered and shook the water off.

'Your name is Carter?' said Wayland.

'Aye. What's it to you?' Carter turned his head towards them, attempting to focus on his captors. 'Who are you?' he said and then, 'Alun? Is it you man? What in God's name are you doing here?'

'Never mind that,' said Alun, 'where's Agnes?'

'Agnes? Oh.'

'Yes, Agnes. My sister in case you've forgotten. I am presuming she's your wife now.' There was a sharp edge to Alun's voice. Carter said nothing but looked down at the ground.

'Well?' said Wayland.

'Look, I'm sorry,' Carter began but his voice seemed to fail.

'Sorry? Sorry for what exactly?' Alun shook him. Wayland stepped forward and slapped the man's face.

'You'll be sorrier if you don't tell us,' he said.

'It was after Naseby,' Carter croaked, 'you did hear about Naseby?'

'The battle there, yes,' replied Wayland, 'when the army thrashed your lot and, from what I heard, your side just upped and ran away."

'Ran away? Did you?' asked Alun, 'And left Agnes behind?'

'No. It wasn't like that. I, we… we had no choice. The army, I've never seen anything like it. So… disciplined. Out-flanked us on every side. Ruthless.' He drooped down again. Alun pulled him up by the chin.

'So you deserted?'

'Don't call it that. I took my chance, that's all. It was that or get… get cut to ribbons.' Carter was talking faster now. 'They say the King lost more than five hundred officers that day. They count the officers, you know, but they don't count the men. I saw with my own eyes there were many more men, shot, slashed, hacked. Me, well, to speak plainly, I joined for the money, for the regular money. Not, well not especially, for the King.' Carter looked round, shaking, as he spoke.

'No–one else is listening,' said Alun, 'so you can carry on.'

'Agnes, well, she was with the women, of course, in the camp behind. So then… then you know.'

'So then we know? So then we know what?'

'So… so I have to suppose she was likely killed. With the others.'

Wayland, remembering Mary's account, had begun to suspect this news but Alun was clearly shocked. Alun sat down suddenly, one hand on his chest. 'Killed?' he said, 'Who by? Who killed her?'

'It was a massacre, from what I heard after.' Carter took a deep breath. Then he told them some of what he'd heard about the massacre of camp followers after the battle's end in Naseby three years back. His account pretty much matched Mary's. Like her, he mentioned the mutilations though not in detail. He stopped short abruptly, remembering his audience.

16.

lun sat on the trough, his face drained of what little colour it had before. 'You're sure?' He asked the question but there was no hope in his voice.

Carter looked up at him, calculating now. 'How can I *know* for *sure*? But...'

'But what?'

'But, I heard it from four different sources.' Carter replied.

Wayland looked up. 'Listen.' he said. They all heard it then. A military drumming, weak and irregular but drawing closer.

'Help me,' said Carter, 'they mustn't find me. I'm done for if they find me.'

'If you think we care one copper farthing for your dirty little neck then you are much mistaken,' Wayland said as he pulled Alun up by his sleeves and shook him. 'Come on, we need to get away from here.'

Leaving the horses by the trough, they moved over to an alley opposite the inn. With some new-found lease of energy, Carter followed. The four of them stood in the shadows, watching as first the infantrymen and then the horse soldiers came into view. The lone drummer was the only real sign that this ragged collection of men was actually still part of an army. Their uniforms were torn and dirtied. Some had no uniform at all. Their pace was a walk rather than a march, despite the best efforts of the drummer. The horses that followed the infantry looked exhausted too, their heads drooping down. Their riders dismounted and walked the horses to the trough. Even the sight of water failed to liven these horses although they did drink. Wayland looked over in the direction of their own horses and was relieved to see that they were just out of sight under the shelter of the trees. He prayed fervently that they were also tired – too tired to whinny when they heard the King's horses.

The soldiers at the front of the line halted outside the inn. Wayland heard the inn doors being bolted against them but he doubted this would hold them for long and so it proved. The soldiers numbered about eighty now, milling around the inn. Several of them thumped on the doors with pike handles. 'Open, in the name of the King.' bellowed one.

There was the sound of bolts being drawn and the woman who'd served Wayland emerged, pulling the door to behind her. She wiped her hands on her skirts, taking her time. Then she struck a defiant pose, arms crossed. 'If

97

you can pay, I will serve you. But my rooms are not large. Seat only some of your men in here and pray you settle the rest out through the back.'

She pointed to the rear of the inn. Wayland thought it was a brave try but he very much doubted she'd see the full tally paid. He watched with relief until the last man had entered the inn. 'Now quick,' he said, 'now's our chance.'

'What about me?' asked Carter.

'You?' Wayland asked, 'Why should we care about you? You were one of them – we're the enemy.'

'And how much did you care about Agnes? Like you, we're just going to look out for us.' Alun added.

'Have you no horse?' Wayland asked. Even at such a time it was second nature to him to think about horses.

'What? No. I'm not one of them now – and so… and so I've no horse,' Carter said.

'Leave him, Wayland.' Alun said.

'Wait,' Carter said, 'Your name is Wayland?'

'What of it?' Wayland said, turning to go.

'You were away last year. And that's your boy?'

Wayland stopped short. 'What do you know of me?'

'Of you? Nothing more. But your wife? Maybe I know something about her you'd likely want to know.'

Wayland reached out, grabbing Carter by the throat. 'What?' he said, 'Have you…'

Shouts from the King's soldiers interrupted him.

'We must go now, right now. Take him if you must, I'm off,' said Alun and he crouched down, ready to sprint across to the horses. Jonathan was already running. Wayland seized hold of Carter's sleeve, pulled him close and set off, dragging him along. They reached the horses without hindrance. Alun and Jonathan untied theirs and mounted. Wayland grabbed Jonathan's reins. 'Sorry, lad,' he said, 'but you're easily the lightest. You'll have to have him.' He hoisted Carter up onto Jonathan's horse to sit behind the boy. He turned to his own horse – only to find she was being held by a King's man.

'Going somewhere?' asked the soldier. Two more men in Royalist uniforms quickly joined him.

'What have we here?' asked one, 'I think Sir Charles will want to know about these suspicious persons, don't you?'

17.

Sir Charles Lucas, it soon turned out, was ensconced in a small clearing just a short way along the road. His men had set up a makeshift table with seating just for him. From the victuals and wine set out it was clear that neither he nor the small entourage of officers on a nearby table had need of any inn. Lucas was not particularly tall but even seated he had a presence. His long, dark brown hair hung down onto his shoulders, teased into curls in the Royalist fashion and in stark contrast to the matted hair of his infantrymen. His moustache, too, was neat and cared for though it did little to disguise the thinness of his lips.

'Well,' he said, 'who have we here?'

Wayland took his cap off and stepped forward. 'Wayland, sir.' he said, 'Blacksmith. Smithing for the horses, that's my trade. This here's my cousin, Alun Jones. The lad is my son Jonathan who helps me, holds the horses and the like.'

Wayland had been careful in his little speech not to name his village and to emphasise the horse aspect of his trade – and not to mention weapon–making. He prayed his luck would hold.

'You are not a soldier then? You have not been fighting against God and the King?' Lucas asked, patting his moustache with a white lace cloth.

'No, sir, God preserve his Majesty. I am a simple smith.' Wayland pulled up his sleeves, revealing a number of scars from furnace burns.

Lucas appeared to consider. He picked up a chicken leg from the small table behind him and held it delicately between two fingers, toying with it. He stared straight at Wayland. He seemed inclined to interrogate him further but just then one of his officers saw his own chance to seize the initiative and perhaps impress Lucas.

'This one, this Jones,' said the officer, 'what does he do?'

'Like the smith said,' said Alun, 'I help with the horses. And, erm, the furnace.'

'Just that?' asked the soldier, sensing Alun's unease, 'I doubt there's much to be earned in that.'

'And... and at times I am a baker. When there's need enough,' he coughed hard, spitting out a mess of floury phlegm.

'And this other one?' Lucas, bored now with Alun, pointed to Carter.

'Nowt to do with us.' Alun said quickly.

'Labourer, sir,' said Carter, 'looking for work, sir.'

'*His* hands don't look like they've seen too much work.' one of Lucas's other officers offered.

'Like I said,' said Carter, 'I am looking for work. I lost my place during the first war. It's hard to make a living in these times.'

'These times,' Lucas said, glowering at Wayland, '*these times* would not be so hard were it not for Cromwell's rabble, overturning the natural order of things.'

Jonathan looked at Wayland. Wayland felt his son's gaze but held his own eyes steady on Lucas.

'No, sir,' he replied calmly, 'that they would not.'

'Well,' said Lucas, absently stroking chicken grease through his moustache, 'I don't suppose now is the time for such philosophising. A smith you say? Well, we have horses. And of course, as it seems obvious to me that if you can fashion shoes from molten iron to any fit I've no doubt that you can make pike points, you can fix muskets and you can do a host of like things we are needing. We have a fair number of weapons that need repairing and I dare say we'll have more before this war's finished. Consider yourself volunteered. We're headed for Colchester.'

'But sir, I implore you, we were going to… I mean, what about my boy…'

But Lucas had turned back to his meal.

18.

$\mathcal{L}$ucas waved a departing hand over towards his left, apparently indicating that one of his officers should deal with the details. Wayland went up to this man but before he could say his piece the man spoke to him.

'The baker's to come whether he will or no. The boy can follow or not follow. That's the choice. But this other one... what's his name?'

Carter stepped forward. 'Wright, sir.' he said just at the very same moment that Wayland said 'Carter.'

'Wright or Carter?' said the officer, scowling, 'Which is it?'

One of his fellow officers went up to Carter, pulled his head up and scrutinised his face. 'I know this one,' he said, 'he was with us at Naseby. At least, he was there at the start. And then he wasn't.' The man spat onto the mud.

'Well then,' said the first one, 'that puts a different light on things. I've no time for a deserter either. And I doubt that Sir Charles Lucas will want him back. He will, though, want to look into this, see if any, ah, justice needs to be, ah, executed.' The soldier smiled at his own joke, but Lucas was now some way off. There was silence for a moment. Carter stared round, looking for an escape route and failing to find one.

'I suppose,' said the officer, 'we will just have to ask Sir Charles later, when we have the chance. So, this man, Carter or Wright, cowardly turd or plain soldier, he comes with us, whether he will or no.' He waved in Carter's direction and a couple of men ran forward, seized hold of Carter and set to tying him up.

A great shouting and drumming proclaimed the end of the soldiers' rest break and men began assembling, ready to march on. Wayland hurried to prepare the horses. 'This screws up everything,' Alun said, 'how are we to find out anything more? Not to mention what about our homes, my bakery – my wife? And your smithy?'

'Well, I do consider it beats being strung up,' Wayland said, his face set grim, 'a little more interrogating and they could have taken us for accomplices, giving succour to a deserter.'

'That bastard has been nothing but trouble since I set eyes on him. If not for him, Agnes would still be alive. And how about what he said about knowing something of your wife?' Alun swivelled round, checking with a glance where Jonathan was and finding him out of earshot before he continued, 'And your boy? What do you think he means?'

'Hush. No time to think like that. We'll bide our time. Things are out of our hands now.'

'Aye', Alun said. 'and that'll only end when this lot wins – or loses outright. We've had some six years of it so far, they lose, they win, we win, we lose and so it goes.'

'Well,' Wayland lowered his voice further, 'let's see when we arrive in the next town. Maybe we can get to Carter, ask him such questions and then slip away.'

'And preferably all without being charged for desertion,' said Alun, glancing round at the soldiers around them.

Wayland thought a while. 'You're the great one for chatting,' he said, 'go find out where exactly we are headed.'

Alun kicked his horse off into a trot. He passed Carter, tied up now and slung onto a supplies wagon, without so much as turning to peer at him. He hesitated, though, before approaching any of the foot soldiers, doubting that any of them would trust him, a man on horseback. He noticed then that one of the horse–soldiers had a horse with a slight limp. 'Hey, friend,' he called, 'has your horse lost a shoe?'

'And what if he has? What's that to you?' the man replied.

'See that man I'm with, him over there?' said Alun, pointing, 'He could fix that. He's a blacksmith.'

'That may be, but I doubt he's got a furnace and spare shoes with him and an hour to spend, now, has he?' the man said. But he looked hopeful despite his cynical reply.

'No, that he's not,' said Alun, 'but he could remove the matching one in short time and then your horse – and you – would be balanced that much better. It might even save your backside a sore old time.'

The man laughed – Alun's point had hit home and he was interested now. He urged his horse over towards Alun and they both steered their mounts towards Wayland. 'Tell me, friend,' Alun continued, 'where are we headed?'

* * *

'Colchester!' Wayland thumped the damp earth where they lay later in that night's camp, further away from the fire than they would have liked, 'Colchester's near the sea.'

'They say,' continued Alun, 'that Sir Charles has his home in Colchester and they hope to raise more troops there.'

'Odd,' said Wayland, 'from what I've heard, Colchester town itself is for Parliament.'

'Home is still home,' Alun pointed out, 'and it wouldn't be the first town divided by these wars. Also, maybe they're expecting help to come in up the river from over the sea. They do say the King has foreign allies.'

'Aye, and his foreign sympathies are part of the problem in this war. But a foreign army? That would be treason to Parliament,' Wayland said, adding half to himself, 'but then to the King, Parliament itself commits treason.'

The journey onwards was uncomfortable but uneventful. A man alone could have covered the ground far more quickly, but this band of king's men was limited to the shuffling speed of its tired foot soldiers and those moving the supply barrows. They had already fled from Kent and most of the infantrymen had, at best, suppurating blisters and such–like persistent hurts and irritations. Wayland and Alun soon found that while they weren't treated as prisoners exactly, they were constantly surrounded and quietly headed off any time one of them tried to veer from the main path. That was not so for Carter. Bound with his hands behind his back he was now roped between two men and chivvied and tugged along none too gently. There was clearly no way either Wayland or Alun would be able to get close to him for now.

The army stopped in Brantry that day. Most of the officers went in to the town centre and, from talk he'd overheard, Alun gathered that Lucas hoped to meet up with other elements of the Royalist army. Wayland's little party was not taken into town but held instead outside until the main group was ready to march on. This was to be the case every time they stopped: their party was kept well away from any contact with the local populace. It was late – about five o'clock on the Monday – when first the hills and then the outer walls of Colchester came into view. There was a mass cursing as they got closer when they saw that the town gates were closed and a band of Colchester's bailiffs and their men were strung out across the London road, barring any entrance.

'By God and by my King,' Lucas shouted, 'we shall pass. We must pass. You will not stop us.' He pushed his horse through to the front of his troops, demanding of the bailiffs' gang that they stand aside. The bailiffs were clearly awed, in part by the obvious and known status of Sir Charles Lucas, and not least by his bearing and angry manner, but they held out nevertheless for two guarantees from the King's men. These were, first, that the rights, liberties and privileges of both the corporation and the inhabitants be secured and secondly that no tax or levy should be demanded of the town. Lucas hesitated at first but after the arrival of a Royalist messenger from the south and some intense conferring with his closest advisers he did concede, fearful that his pursuers were closer now. The bailiffs finally caused the gate to be opened to them – and closed again behind them.

The next few hours were taken up by a great deal of activity. The best quarters were sought out and appropriated for Lucas himself and his immediate cohorts of course. His actual home and manor house was situated outside the city walls and so considered less safe in the circumstances. A disorganised scramble began for living quarters for everyone else. Alun was separated from Wayland and ordered to the town's bakery. Lucas had let it be known that, as the town was known to favour Parliament, he didn't want to run the risk of either himself or his men being poisoned by the town baker or other food suppliers. Wayland was sent to take over the main smithy and to collect whatever supplies he would need to run it, whether for horse shoes or for weapons. There was no sign of the town's own blacksmith and Wayland knew better than to enquire about him. Two soldiers were assigned to help him in his task. Wayland guessed correctly that they would also be charged with ensuring his compliance with the orders. There was, as it happened, a goodly supply of iron and tools, plus he still had his own travelling kit, including two sets of bellows. There was little though in the way of charcoal or other fuel for the furnace. He pointed this out to his guardians.

'Look, I need charcoal. I'll go check with the baker. Bakers always have need of fuel too.' he said, seizing the excuse to seek Alun out. Neither soldier dissented out loud – but it was clear that they were suspicious of his true motives and that he was not going to be allowed out of the smithy alone. 'Bakers must fire up their furnaces – and you'll be wanting fresh–baked bread soon enough, I'll warrant,' he added. This last comment had the desired effect and both men followed Wayland out and along the street. They found Alun arguing loudly with a burly, flour-specked man who was clearly Colchester's town baker. Alun had also been given a king's man to watch over him but his man seemed uninterested. Wayland listened to the two bakers as they traded mild insults and justifications. One of Wayland's guards noticed some knobs of hard bread stuck to the insides of several pans in the corner and soon all three guards crowded round, picking at the still–hot, brittle lumps. Wayland caught a wink from Alun aimed at the other baker – a wink that was returned. They continued their loud debate but began at the same time a quieter exchange, while their guards were distracted.

'I'm thinking you might be none too pleased at this takeover by the king's men,' Alun said in a hushed voice to the other baker, 'but I'm not part of it.'

'You're right there,' said the other, smiling now but adding 'BASTARD!' for the benefit of the guards.

'I'm Alun. This here's Wayland, blacksmith, and he's no king's man neither. BASTARD YOURSELF!'

'Rowland,' said the other baker, 'YOU GOATISH FOOL-BORN LAYABOUT.'

'We've little choice but to go along with them – for now,' Wayland said. Then raising his voice, he added 'I SAID CHARCOAL, AND I WANT IT NOW, YOU FEN-SUCKED LOUT...'

One of the guards looked round, finally concerned.

'ALL RIGHT, ALL RIGHT,' Rowland said and giving Alun another wink, he began stuffing lumps of charcoal in a sack. 'You can find me here or two doors down,' he hissed.

Alun, Wayland and the guards returned to the town forge with the charcoal and Wayland set about firing up the furnace. Once they were out of earshot from the guards, Wayland and Alun talked over their position. 'We have to find Carter.' Wayland said.

'Do you think he will give you any proper answers?'

'I do,' Wayland, 'but how did you read him? Did it sound to you that somehow he could truly know something about Rebecca's...Rebecca's death? Or just that he knew Rebecca somehow?'

'Don't think too much on it,' Alun advised, 'more likely he's just heard something of it and was aiming to get your attention, get you on side to save his miserable skin. You have got to admit, if that was his aim, it worked.'

Wayland smashed the bellows down on to the shelf, but he decided not to argue. They were quiet a while. 'Reckon Rowland might be a useful ally?' asked Wayland to change the subject.

'Aye. Seemed a good sort,' said Alun, 'he was alert, caught on quick enough. I wouldn't be trusting anyone here too much too soon though. Nevertheless, we shall be needing more than one more on our side soon enough, I'll wager.'

Wayland did not reply but he had no doubt that Alun was right. He couldn't foresee how the King's men's occupation of Colchester might play out. But he felt sure there would be some bloody outcome or another before they left the town.

19.

ayland had been up the next day and working since daylight, some seven hours ago, when he heard a great commotion. Watchmen – both from the town and Lucas's force – were shouting and running back and forth with messages. Word quickly spread that a substantial Parliamentary force had been sighted. Lucas readied his men for a fight but instead there appeared an emissary from the Parliamentary side, kitted out with the traditional drum and trumpet to ensure safe passage. His message, which he stressed was from General Fairfax himself, offered assurances that there would be neither bloodshed nor plunder if the King's men should lay down their arms at this point. The bailiffs, of course, were all for it, though they were careful to avoid expressing any explicit support for the Parliamentary cause.

Lord Norwich, who had brought his own supporters to Colchester and who of course out-ranked Lucas, reacted with a robust rejection of Fairfax's offer. Their brief respite in Colchester seemed to have reinvigorated the King's men and now, far from being the dishevelled fugitive band they had seemed while they were on the road, the officers at least appeared more than eager to take on the enemy with force. Wayland and Alun watched developments from on top of a high segment of the town wall. First the trumpeter made his slow and dignified way back to re-join the Parliamentary army. Then, after a short pause for readying their arms, the Royalist horse soldiers sallied out at a gallop onto the London Road followed shortly afterwards by the infantry. Both forces paused to stare eye to eye at their opposites but very soon the soldiers of both sides were fighting hand to hand, with pike and sword. Alun groaned at each small victory or loss but Wayland held his tongue. A Parliamentary victory *ought* to see them freed but he knew there could be danger too, for himself, Alun and the boy from an over-zealous army invading the town if Fairfax failed to impose a tight enough discipline on his men.

In the end, as it came to dusk, it became clear that neither side had secured an outright victory. General Fairfax simply ordered the retreat sounded and his forces began to withdraw from inside the city walls. Noting the demeanour of the soldiers and recognising it from his own army days, Wayland turned to Alun. 'Watch them,' he said, 'their mood has turned.'

Wayland was right enough. Fairfax's men turned on the townspeople on their way out, venting their frustration and anger, threatening and robbing as they went, with no thought given to the common people – even though Colchester's inhabitants were well known to support Parliament. Worse, Wayland saw smoke rising from the thatches of several small houses. The sound of women wailing soon followed the soldiers as they made their ragged march away from Colchester. 'At least they're gone.' said Alun.

'But the King's men will be back here soon enough,' Wayland said, 'so we'd best hurry back.'

He and Alun scrambled back down from the wall to make their way back to the town's centre so as to be seen at their respective workplaces before they were missed. They stood to one side as the king's men overtook them. First, through the little street, towards the main stabling block and from the direction of the gate, came the higher-ranking horse soldiers. In high spirits, they passed Wayland without so much as a glance and Wayland for his part was careful to avoid looking in their direction. A familiar voice caught his attention though, as the horse soldiers came through next. At the same moment, Alun, who'd hung back, pressed into the doorway behind Wayland, jabbed him in the back. 'Look who it is! Would you believe that?'

The familiar voice had come from Carter. Carter was mounted on a large-boned black horse and his bearing now was utterly different from when they had last seen him: he looked and sounded confident, jaunty almost. He gazed directly at Wayland, spat in his direction and kicked his horse on past. Next to pass through were the foot soldiers and the wounded. Wayland stood back, to indicate a respect for the injured that he felt instinctively, as a former soldier himself. He and Alun finally reached the safety of the smithy.

'Tell me that wasn't Carter,' said Alun.

'It was though.'

'The slimy bastard! How did he wangle that? He's not just free. They've given him a horse. He must have cleaned up his act in short time – and talked himself back into favour.'

'Shh,' said Wayland, 'not so loud.' But he too was dismayed at Carter's transformation. If it was difficult to get at him before, it would now be more difficult, and it would be more dangerous.

That night there was a great deal of carousing by the Royalist leaders. They might not have won any battle but they were clearly determined to celebrate not losing. Wayland soon discovered that in addition to Sir Charles Lucas and Lord Norwich there were two other Lords: Lord Loughborough and Lord Capel, plus two further knights: Sir George Lisle and Sir Bernard Gascoigne. As far as Wayland could tell from the gossip he overheard, these gentlemen were, for the most part, more used to life in their grand country homes than to battle, other than occasional low-key skirmishes. More than that, though, he was fairly sure that most of their men, the ordinary soldiers, seemed to be pressed men, forced from their daily lives of crop tending and the like to fight for the King. That had been true also of the Parliamentary forces at the beginning of the civil war and during Wayland's time in their service. Wayland himself had, of course, been a pressed man. Now though, he'd heard that Cromwell had refined and trained his all men. There were some who called it a "Model"

Army now, such was the discipline and effectiveness of the Parliamentary Army. Wayland had heard that Cromwell's men even received regular pay and, though he guessed that was probably an exaggeration, he knew that money was often a better motivator for the ordinary man than any less tangible consideration of loyalty. Especially as this was now a flare-up of a civil war that had already exhausted many men's initial enthusiasm. The King's enemy would be a greater force to be reckoned with than it was last time.

What happened in the days that followed, though, was not the bloody battle and defeat that Wayland feared. Instead his immediate worries were replaced by a more continuous, on-going anxiety. The town walls echoed at night with the sounds, albeit distant, of digging and building works. Rumours and counter-rumours circulated constantly and quickly but most of them pointed to the same conclusion: the Parliamentary forces were making trenches and rough fortifications, preparing for a lengthy, old style siege. Wayland overheard Lucas and Norwich discussing this one evening. Both men were upbeat, even away from their men. He learnt soon after, from one of the foot soldiers, that the reason for their confidence of was the expectation that help was expected imminently from the south and that further assistance should be forthcoming in the form of a distraction as the Scots and northern Royalist forces would be engaging the Parliamentary army elsewhere. Wayland had no way of knowing, of course, how effective any such help might be, whether it would or could be waylaid by Parliamentary forces or if in fact there was any such help to be had. He had heard, though, from fellow soldiers during his time in the army, about the tactics used in some great siege on the continent. He couldn't remember where – in the Low Countries perhaps – but it had lasted months. Hundreds – some said thousands – of those trapped within had succumbed to starvation. Still, he couldn't see Fairfax waiting months. Either some reinforcement would indeed arrive to relieve the King's side or more likely, Fairfax would blast his way through the town walls. Still, the siege might well last a couple of weeks. He thought through the likely trajectory of a siege. He estimated that Lucas's force must total about 3,000 men, bringing with them presumably well over a thousand horses in addition to those already in the town. Horses have large appetites. Animal feed would likely run out first.

Partly out of concern for his own two horses, but also in consideration of all the horses now confined within the town centre, he decided now to start up a basic numbering, an inventory of the available animal feed. He quickly found it wanting. On each of his charcoal–seeking missions, he began to set aside some animal food for his own horses. Then he began to look out for the actual and potential food sources for all souls within the town walls, rich and poor, king's men or simple townsfolk. Of course, it all depended on a great many assumptions. He knew, for example, that the army horses were usually fed a lot more than ordinary workhorses like his. He doubted that the cavalry would take straightaway to any rationing. As to people, Rowland, the local baker, had put the number of townspeople at some eight thousand. With an estimated three thousand king's men plus those few camp followers who'd come through the town gates with them that would take the total to easily over eleven thousand souls. He guessed that Lucas would soon attempt to make sallies out to raid for supplies and, at the moment, it looked as though the river route via the Hythe might still be used if anyone outside were prepared to trade with them. Wayland was cautious by nature. As a smith, of course, he'd had no land or crops of his own to rely on and so he was used to planning ahead and storing food. He very much doubted that either Lucas or the other Royalist leaders had even begun to see the magnitude of the problem, so confident were they of relief from the expected reinforcements.

The next few days passed quietly enough. Despite Wayland's dim view of the King's men's planning capabilities, a contingent of infantrymen had, in fact, been ordered to search throughout the town, commandeering supplies and forcing their will upon a surly population. All corn, in particular, was requisitioned and brought into a central storage area and all meat or dairy animals were commandeered. Alun, meanwhile, was dismayed to learn that in their vengeful retreat the Parliamentary forces had smashed even the town's two millstones. He and Rowland assembled all the ready-milled flour they could find and took it in turns to guard the sacks. The persistent rain added to the townspeople's low mood. Although it was midsummer for day after day the cloud cover brought an earlier end to daylight than was properly due. At night, however, the officers continued to eat well – and to drink better. From his hay-strewn loft next to the smithy, Wayland could hear them carousing every night.

One positive consequence of the now settled-in siege was that with the town gates closed and given the lack of any obvious escape route, both Wayland and Alun found that they were guarded much less closely. While it was a welcome development that their guards tended to stand further off, talking amongst themselves and showing little interest in the few conversations that Wayland managed to snatch with Alun, they were both thwarted from their aim of questioning Carter by the simple fact that the guards were still actually present. Also, they had yet to discover where Carter was billeted. Wayland found too that, with his guards keeping more distance, he had fewer opportunities to overhear discussions that might give them more insight into what was planned, what was expected and what was feared by the King's men. Nevertheless, it was clear that reinforcements were still expected, though Wayland had no real feel for whether these would actually come or when they might be expected.

He continued to work the furnace, outwardly calm and steady. At first he mostly fixed shoeing problems for Lucas' men's horses but as he worked, the pile of ironware – generally weapons requiring small but fiddly repairs – grew and grew. He felt an increasing anxiety that Lucas would send one of his key men chasing after these, but he was still loath to assist the king's men with weapons. After all, they would be aimed at the Parliamentary side, the side on which he himself had fought, albeit with no option. Much as he considered that he had nothing but contempt for the rhetoric of both sides he found his underlying sympathies remained with the Parliamentary army. He was worried, too, about how he and the boy could get away unscathed. Jonathan was not reacting well to their confinement. He seemed, if it were possible, even more withdrawn than before. Wayland gave him as much work with horses as he could. He soon persuaded a couple of the king's horsemen to let the boy help out with their horses. Jonathan had been disappointed at first that the kind of horse favoured by the king's army was not, as he had imagined, the mighty destrier of a medieval knight. Wayland explained to him that since modern war involved the use of canons it necessarily required a more nimble mount. Still, these horses were far superior to the farm horses the boy had generally worked with before. Their faces had the attractive dished nose that hints at some small element of Arab ancestry. Jonathan found too that the soldiers' horses, when properly fed, were a great deal livelier than the horses he was used to, but he soon adapted his ways with them and they seem to respond well to his gentle, if silent, approach.

Wayland's drive to catch the killer remained. Fear got in its way. Worry about Jonathan got in its way. His heavy workload and the constant need to find, prepare and share food with Alun and Jonathan got in its way. But the desire to track down the killer was a given constant behind all his thoughts and all his actions – even if he was never really sure if he was seeking out the boy's killer, his wife's killer or both. With no other clues, his fevered mind always came back to Carter. The man must know something. Finding out what the something was might be a start, a thread to pull to begin a bigger unravelling. He looked constantly for ways to get out, to find out about him and to get close enough to the man. Perhaps, he thought, Alun, being less closely guarded, was more likely to be able to seize an opportunity to reach Carter and to interrogate him. Alun had motive enough too to do it and Wayland was confident that he'd be dogged enough to keep at it. He fretted though that Alun on his own wouldn't be sufficient – now that Carter's fortunes seemed to have been so far reversed. So, in the end he concluded that they'd both need to get to Carter some time when the man was not accompanied by fellow soldiers. If the Parliamentary army broke the siege and managed to capture the town, all would be chaos and the chances were that Carter would be taken and therefore out of Wayland's reach. Conversely, if the King's supporters arrived, defeated the Parliamentary army and succeeded in relieving the King's men, the chances were that Carter would leave in triumph. In either case, getting to Carter would be out of Wayland's control in the longer term. But in the shorter term there was no obvious way to get to him either. Wayland, however, was prepared to risk everything. As he'd told Alun, revenge drove him like a thirst.

20.

Leicester, June 1645

About twenty Parliamentary infantrymen were drinking heavily in the alehouse. Nehemiah, one of them and yet as always alone, cradled his ale and strained to listen to them. His hand went instinctively to his left ear, briefly touched the jagged edge where part of the ear was missing. The talk was all about Irish atrocities and snatches of their talk rose above the general loud buzz:

'For a start, the Irish are heretics...'

'Traitors too. 'Tis well known that they support the ...'

'Just a few years back, it was, when them murdering bastards killed thousands...'

'tens of thousands I heard...'

'of English Protestants...

'aye, they're all at it, women and wee children too...'

Nehemiah, taking a sip, reflected on how their talk had changed since the immediate aftermath of the massacre at Naseby. Standing on bodies, their faces running with sweat and blood spatter, it had all been about triumph and boasting then.

'Did you see that whore? I marked her good and proper...'

'Well, she'll not be whoring again in this life...'

'True. Still her face will tell St Peter now to send her to the fires...'

'I reckon I got three of them...'

'I got five...'

Nehemiah hadn't joined in their jubilation of blood lust then and, he thought to himself, he certainly wasn't about to join in their noisy need for justifications now. He felt so very different from them. He had no need to summon up reasons for what he'd done. What he liked to do was to revisit in his thoughts, in calm times, the moments, the actual acts of what he'd done. Only his own acts. Not so for the rest of them. Where they had slashed wildly, looked to the next one and moved on, he'd taken it slowly. Enjoyed – yes, relished it all. Watching that one's eyes when he slit into her face. Seeing the change in another one's eyes when the knife finally left her breasts to slide slowly through that soft belly. Feeling the hot breath of her gasps and looking into her wide-awake stare when he twisted the blade. It was always at that last moment when their faces would merge into the face of that first woman, the one he'd failed to kill, the one who ripped at his ear and fled.

Nehemiah shifted on his stool, to hide better the movement in his breeches. Fast as his fellow soldiers were justifying their own actions and distancing themselves from the carnage, he was savouring his memories – and wondering: when would he find such moments again?

21.

Colchester, 1648

An opportunity – or more accurately, some slight chance of an opportunity – to find out more about Carter and his change of fortune did arise the following Monday. Lucas had called for all able-bodied men under his command – three were excused by reason of the leg injuries they had received in that first battle – to assemble in front of the castle. 'In case you hadn't worked it out, that includes us. And for that reason of necessity it includes you two as well.' one of Wayland's guards instructed him with some relish.

Two officers on horseback rode around the square, picking out men. One of those officers was Carter himself. He looked over the men grouped around him. His gaze skipped quickly over Wayland and Alun, but he pointed at them nevertheless and signalled for them to join his little party. 'What's up?' Wayland asked of the man next to him as they all set off in the direction of the river, the one town boundary that wasn't yet blocked to the besieged by Fairfax's siege men.

'Seems we're off to the Hythe, to search for and fetch in supplies.' was the reply.

'Supplies of what?' Alun asked, 'Nothing too heavy, I hope.' A coughing fit overtook him just at the thought of lifting stuff.

'What's up with him?' one man asked Wayland.

'I'm coughing – I'm not dumb,' Alan said sharply, 'and respecting your profession and all, but I'm not a soldier. I'm a baker.'

'All right, take it easy. I didn't volunteer either as it happens.'

'How long have you been with the King's army, then?' asked Wayland, hoping to get the man on side.

'Only a matter of weeks,' he replied.

'That's not long – but it is longer than we have been, swept up with them. I expect you've learnt the set-up here? What's this Hythe? A village? And d'you know him, that one over there?' Wayland pointed at Carter who was some twenty feet away, riding up and down the front of the line of men.

'Well, the Hythe, now that's an easy one. It's the town's quay. It's the loading and unloading point for goods to and from the merchants' ships. But as to him... now, if you'd asked me about anyone but him I could tell you. But that one? It's a bit of a mystery, to me at least. One minute he's a prisoner. Next thing, Lisle comes in to see him. Sir

George Lisle no less. Five minutes later, he's not just freed but lording it over us. It's always the same. It depends on who you know. Doesn't matter so much what you've done.'

'Aye,' said Wayland and they left it at that, for at that moment a cry went up. The men furthest from them had discovered a huge stash of goods on the quayside. Wayland and Alun went over there to see. There were great sacks of wheat, barley, salt, spice – and some powder that turned out on further inspection to be gunpowder.

'Gifts as a great Providence!' one man was moved to shout.

'This find must surely tide us over until such time as the relief forces arrive.' exclaimed another. Many of the men were whooping as if to signify their agreement.

'If indeed any relief is to make it here.' said Wayland but he said it quietly, for only Alun to hear.

They walked further out, along from the inner ramparts, passing several buildings hit by Parliamentary canons. Women and children swarmed over the rubble, snatching up anything that might conceivably be useful to the besieged: wood for the fires, anything that could be eaten, iron for forging weapons. They looked round constantly as they worked, in dread of further bombardments. Wayland nudged Alun.

'Over there! Is that what I think it is?'

There was a semi–circle of stone showing amongst some fallen timbers. Alun hurried over to it. He pulled away the small stones and wood covering the rest of it. 'Yes!' he shouted back.

Carter must have heard him for he looked up and kicked his horse to canter over to Alun.

'What's all your fuss about?' Carter didn't look impressed, 'what can our forces do with that old stone? Do you think we might throw it from the city walls onto the enemy, like some old Roman? Is that the best you've got?'

'It's a millstone,' said Wayland, 'it has considerable value now: with the mills gone, destroyed by Fairfax's men on their way out of here, we've none left within the walls.'

Carter just stared.

'The flour,' said Alun, 'we need it to make flour.'

There was a pause. 'All right – but how shall it turn? Are we to build a windmill for you now?' Carter's tone was more confident again, his voice rising with sarcasm.

'We can rig up a pulley for a horse to turn it. Wayland will know how to fashion one.' said Alun.

Carter said nothing it at first. Maybe he didn't like being shown up as ignorant in front of his men. 'We'll take it then,' he said eventually, jabbing at his horse with his spurs, 'and you –' he turned to Alun, 'you can bring it in. And that's an order'

Alun looked at Wayland but went nevertheless to pull at one of the timbers pinning the stone down – and fell straightaway into a coughing fit.

'Don't be daft, man, he can't shift that.' Wayland shouted across the way.

Carter looked round and wrenched his horse into a tight turn. He trotted over to Wayland. 'He – and you – can and shall follow my orders. Or he can take the consequences.' he said.

'It needs a horse and cart, clear as day.' said Wayland, 'I'll send for one.'

'No horse that belongs to our King will pull a cart.' Carter said with such viciousness that the men near to him stopped working and stared. Noticing that, Carter rode right up to Wayland, drew his sword and rested it on Wayland's shoulder. 'I could have your throat slit, or I could do it myself, right now,' he said, his voice a harsh hiss.

A thin line of red trickled down Wayland's neck but he stood still, ignoring the sword. He stared back at Carter. 'You're singing a different tune today.' he remarked.

Carter's neck muscles tensed and his cheeks flushed red. 'I have connections here,' Carter said finally, 'and you'd do well to remember that.'

'Oh, I will, don't you worry – for now. Maybe when this…' Wayland waved his arm in the general direction of the town walls, 'is all over, then *you* can start to worry. Unless you'd like to finish telling me now what it was you were going to tell me back at the alehouse.'

Carter pulled the sword back, went to sheath it, changed his mind and slapped his horse with the flat blade. The horse jerked straight into a canter.

Wayland watched Carter go.

'I thought for one minute he was going to knight you, what with that sword on the shoulder thing.' said Alun, loud enough that a couple of nearby soldiers laughed. Alun waited until they'd all settled back into sorting through the mess of stone and timber. He turned to Wayland. 'We'll have to watch our back with him, mind you, let alone worry about getting to him. And now, what do we do now?'

'Right now,' said Wayland, 'now we get a horse and cart to pull home that millstone. You can take a break from shifting stuff and amble back into the centre. Borrow – and I *am* saying *borrow* not *take* – a cart from someone in the town. Be courteous about it too – we need the townsfolk on our side and they'll be riled up already, what with the Parliamentarians burning their homes and this lot taking just whatever they fancy. When you have the cart, go get Jonathan and have him harness up my mare and bring the cart here. Then we'll rope up the millstone, maybe get some of those men over there to help. Maybe we can just roll the it up on to the cart with a flat slab of wood and we're away.'

'Amble?' said Alun, spluttering, 'Yes, I think I can manage an amble. The town baker, Rowland, should likely have a flour cart – stashed away somewhere by now if I know bakers.' He started to set off back into the town but turned back. 'When we've finished with that great stone,' he began.

'Finished with it? How do you mean? You'll not be finished having to grind out flour till the Parliamentary Army's done besieging.' said Wayland.

'When we've finished,' Alun repeated, 'I can think of a neck we can tie it to. Then we can try his idea of tipping it over the city walls.'

Wayland grunted and turned back to sorting through the rubble. But he did take some brief pleasure from his fleeting vision of Carter, thrown into some fast-moving river with that millstone weighing him down.

22.

ayland woke with a start. He shook his head, trying to clear from it the remnants of his usual nightmare involving the witnessing of one of Rebecca's many deaths, in horrendous detail, himself powerless. He knew that some sound had wakened him. Now he strained to hear what it was. Outside there was the barest hint of a dawn to come. It was too late, then, for the usual carousing to have woken him, even if the Royalist officers had had some really good reason to celebrate. The usual disturbance from Fairfax's men as they constructed yet more fortifications in the dark, so as to avoid the muskets and canons of the King's men, had ceased in recent nights. Wayland guessed that they had moved on, away from his side of the town. So what could it have been then? A brawl? No, not that – for then it came again, and he knew it now for a woman's voice, that of a woman in fear. He waited, hoping it would stop.

When it didn't, he reached for his breeches, pulled them on and padded, shoeless, to the door. Last night, he and Alun had been talking late, past their unofficial curfew time and Alun had stayed over in the smithy rather than risk the ire of the King's Men patrolling. He looked over now to Alun's makeshift bed. He saw him stir but then utter some kind of grunt and roll over. Wayland left him there and ventured out. He trod carefully between the solid lumps of sleeping men on the floor in the main room beyond his and went out into the street. He paused to listen. The woman's cry came again, higher pitched and sounding more desperate. It came, he reckoned, from the third or fourth hovel along the street. He gave a quick glance behind him but there was no sign of anyone else awake. The noise got louder as he neared the last house in the row, but Wayland didn't run. Instead, he slowed to a halt by its window. There seemed to be a faint light on in the house. Perhaps it was candle–light from an adjoining room, thought Wayland. He strained his eyes to see into the house. Nothing. Then he heard a man's grunt followed by the sound of a fist hitting flesh. The woman's cries had turned to sobs now.

'Lie still, you whore,' hissed a man's voice, 'I'll be at your manky pole–hole whether you will or no.'

Wayland felt his heart race as his reflexes kicked in and his mind filled with violence. Later, he did wonder if his reactions would have been so quick and so extreme if he had not so recently dreamt of Rebecca. And if he'd not thought he recognised the man's voice: Carter. Yes, it was Carter, no doubt. Wayland had both a strong feeling for justice and a general inclination to protect women and children. He was a father and he'd been a husband. But maybe the truth was that it was his lust for revenge that was driving him right now. He hurled himself at the door again and again until it splintered and cracked in two. He took in the scene in an instant. Carter had the woman on the floor. Her skirt and petticoats were up, his breeches were down – and he had a knife at her exposed breast. Blood trickled from the knifepoint across the whiteness of her skin.

'What in God's name…' Carter began as he caught sight of Wayland.

'God?' Wayland shouted, '*You* have the nerve to call on God?'

Carter stood up. 'You?' he said. He started to pull his breeches up with one hand, but Wayland hit him before he finished, knocking the knife out of his other hand. The woman scrabbled back, away from the two men and shrank into a corner. Wayland was shouting: rapid, meaningless insults, each one accompanied by his fist smashing into Carter's chest. Carter broke away. 'Have her, then,' said Carter, panting and trying again to fix his breeches, 'take her.'

'What? That's not…' Shocked, Wayland paused for a moment.

Carter looked straight at him. 'Oh yes, he said, 'I know. The wife. The little woman at home. You still love her. But wait a moment. Isn't she dead?'

Wayland's mouth dropped open. His rage surged up again. He launched himself at Carter and they crashed to the ground. Years of manual work with molten iron had given Wayland's arms great strength but Carter's arms were longer and he was able to fight back while keeping his face further away. He spat, too, momentarily blinding Wayland with phlegm. Seizing his advantage, he held off Wayland with one hand while with the other he pulled a short dagger from his breeches. He brought its serrated blade up, closer and closer towards Wayland's neck, grunting all the while with effort and triumph.

Wayland heard a loud howl and felt his face hit by shards of something. Carter's grip had gone limp and Wayland was able to pull back and wipe his eyes clear. As the room came back into focus, he saw that Carter was lying on the floor, his head bleeding. Lumps of broken pot lay around him. The woman was still holding the remnants of the pot's handles. They both looked down at Carter. He lay unconscious on the floor, his bottom exposed, the breeches around his knees again. The woman stepped forward and kicked at Carter's inert form.

'I think he's out, for now,' said Wayland, 'thanks to you!'

'And some thanks due to you, I think, that I am not out!' she said smiling at Wayland, 'Well, I'm Alice. And you are?'

'Wayland.' he said, momentarily lost for more words.

'I am Tom the weaver's widow,' she continued, 'and this is my home.' She waited and when Wayland said nothing she smiled again. He thought she looked very different when she smiled. But she would of course, since the danger had passed. 'So, my question now, I suppose, is,' she said, 'who is Wayland? I mean, I take it that you're not from Colchester. Where are you from? And what are you?'

'Please excuse my manners,' he said, 'I'm a blacksmith. My smithy is for horses not weapons though – when I've a say in it. Which, come to think of it, has not been the case at all since I've been caught up here in this damned siege.' He thought then that perhaps he was becoming too garrulous, so he stopped. He only realised much later that he'd not really explained anything nor mentioned what had first set him on the road that had led to Colchester: Rebecca and the search for the boy's killer.

Alice brought a cloth and wiped his face. As she took the cloth to put it down, he saw her kick Carter again as she passed. Carter twitched a little but he didn't return to consciousness. Wayland and Alice gazed at each other, seemingly frozen in time. Neither of them noticed Alun walk in through the broken door until he spoke. 'Wayland! Here you are. You must come back now.' Alun stared around the room. 'Oh no,' he said, taking in Carter's exposed nether parts, 'you've been rescuing maidens and getting yourself into trouble again.'

He saw then the blood seeping from Carter's head wound. 'Oh, Lord!'

'It's all right,' said Wayland, 'or at least, it's not as bad as you might think. He's not dead.'

Alice kicked Carter again to see him twitch and prove the point.

'Well, I suppose that's something. But you're lucky I've found you first,' Alun said, 'you've made enough noise between you to raise all the King's men. Come now and be quick, before we all get caught.'

'You can't leave that here,' said Alice, pointing at Carter.

'No, that's for sure,' said Wayland, 'and we shall not.'

'It's "we" now, is it?' said Alun with a sigh. But he bent down with Wayland and they each took one of Carter's legs. They dragged him on his back out through the doorway and along past six or seven houses. Then they pushed him into the drainage gulley beside the street.

'Move his head,' said Alun, 'or he'll drown in piss when folks wake and empty out their pisspots.'

They lifted his head onto the side walkway. Wayland checked Carter's chest quickly for its heartbeat and breathing movement. 'He'll wake. Not that I give one damnation in hell, but I do mind about such a commotion as his death could cause.'

'What about the commotion he'll cause when he tells?' said Alun.

'Tells what? That I stopped him raping a town resident. And that after Sir Charles gave his word to the people and to Colchester's finest that not a single town resident would be touched? Think about it. His fellow officers will likely put it all – his appearance and his night out – down to drink. And he'll likely let them.'

'Maybe,' said Alun, doubtful, 'but he'll still be mad as hell with you.'

'Let him,' said Wayland, 'I'm more than a little mad with *him*. Now wait here a moment.' Wayland went back to Alice's house. He knocked on the broken doorframe. She beckoned him in and he went over to her. 'I must leave, it seems.'

She nodded, looking him in the eyes. 'My thanks again,' she said.

He started to reach out to touch her hand but held back suddenly and ended up patting her elbow.

'Happen I'll be back,' he paused before continuing, 'else you can find me, some time, either in the smithy or else in the baker's place. That was the baker who came in, see, he's a friend of mine.'

She nodded but said nothing.

'Here,' he said, stepping outside and pulling the bulk of the splintered door upright and over to the open doorway, 'If I prop this against the door frame, it'll do till dawn. I'll see to it that it's fixed in the morning. Folk might talk if I'm seen fixing it now.'

He went back to Alun and they made their way back to their meagre lodgings. Alun was clearly curious about Wayland's actions but he got little explanation. 'I heard the screams. I went; it seemed obvious what needed to be done.' was all Wayland said.

'The gallant smith rescues another maiden,' Alun said, with a sing-song tone, 'despite the trouble the last one got him into...'

He stopped short, catching a glower from Wayland.

'The thing is,' said Wayland, later, as they parted, 'the more important thing is that I needed him – Carter – alive. I've still had no answer from him on what he knows about Rebecca.'

'If anything,' said Alun.

'Aye, if anything. But I *will* find out.'

'If he doesn't have you killed or jailed first.'

23.

Wayland collected a few tools and took Jonathan round to Alice's place the next day. He had thought at first that the lad might be curious as to how he'd come to meet a woman overnight. He didn't tell him anything about it though. He always had at the back of his mind the hope that maybe one day there'd be something so compelling that Jonathan would want to know about so much that he'd start talking again in order to get an answer. But when he broached their mission with Jonathan the boy simply nodded.

Alice was up and ready when they arrived. Wayland noticed that she was wearing a different dress and her hair was neatly pinned under a plain bonnet. He thought he could smell rosewater on her hair. She welcomed Jonathan when Wayland introduced him and offered him a small, plain oatcake, apologising that she'd nothing else to give him. She raised an eyebrow when the boy simply nodded and smiled. Wayland sent him off to look a couple of streets away for some broken pieces of wood he'd spied the day before. Then he thanked her on Jonathan's behalf, explaining that his son hadn't spoken since his mother's death.

'Ah.' she said simply. Neither of them mentioned the previous night's events and Wayland began preparing the door for repair by propping it into place. He patched it up, hammering on the pieces of wood that Jonathan brought back. When he and the boy went to leave, she held his gaze for a moment.

'If,' he said, 'I mean, well, suppose, if the door doesn't hold for any reason – though it should be firm enough – but if not, well, you can find me, like I said, most times at the smithy.'

She smiled. She looked at the solid patchwork on the door, held in place as it was by large iron nails. 'I wager it'll hold,' she said, 'and I thank you both.'

'But still...' he looked straight into her eyes. Green, he noted. He let his words hang there a moment. Then he turned and left.

Wayland thought of Alice many times over the next three days, but she didn't turn up at the smithy and the king's men kept him busy with more and more demands for weapon repairs and gave him no opportunity to pass by her house. Despite the huge finds of supplies at the Hythe quay, the situation seemed to have eased very little for the ordinary townspeople. The king's men had commandeered all the sacks and, although there had been some nominal small distributions via the town's bailiffs,

Wayland was aware that very little food had reached most citizens. His own position was somewhere between the adequate food stocks enjoyed by the officers and the desperate scarcities inflicted on the majority. He was given – at irregular intervals it's true – a basic allowance of strips of dried meat, since money payments were rapidly being replaced in the town by bartering due to the distorted values of food under siege. Thanks to Alun, Wayland also had access to the crusty bits of bread left on the oven walls after each morning's baking. Such morsels were actually the best parts of the loaves made now. He knew that Alun was reduced to bulking up the bread mix with the addition of sweepings of flour and dust of doubtful nutritional value. Wayland didn't like to consider how much was dust compared with how much was flour, but he knew such sweepings tended to sink to the middle of the dough mix. Now, whenever he thought as he worked the molten iron and whenever he tossed and turned on his rough pallet, hoping to sleep, two further issues tended to crowd his mind, vying with his morbid thoughts of Rebecca: Carter and the matter of what he knew or didn't know and Alice and whether or how he could take her some scraps of food.

At first, after his fight with Carter, he'd worried, too, despite his own bold talk, that Alun's warning was right, that the man would have worked his boasted contacts, pulled strings to make trouble for Wayland with the king's men. When nothing seemed to come of it, though, he let go of that worry and so his other worries loomed larger. On the fourth day after his fight, however, there were developments, albeit slight, on both counts. He overheard one of the king's men mention that Carter was lying up in the army's makeshift injury room. He was said to be recovering from some accident he'd had with a horse. The first problem was that in this building there were, of course, several other wounded king's men being treated for musket or canon shot. There seemed to be no obvious way he could get at Carter.

That same day, he had a large job lot of weapons to repair, by personal order of Sir Charles Lucas and with it a promise of 'a goodly meal when you're done with it.' He worked away at his furnace with rather more enthusiasm than was his wont, finishing only after dark. His reward duly arrived, but Wayland was disappointed to find that he still couldn't leave the smithy without the company of a guard. He sent Jonathan instead to Alice, with a parcel comprising nearly all of the meat he'd been given plus a couple of chunks of bread. There was of course no point in quizzing the boy on his return. Wayland's simple 'All right?' to him had elicited a nod though.

A couple of days later the distraction of a messenger from Fairfax to the Royalist commanders did provide Wayland with the opportunity he'd been waiting for. He slipped out of the smithy while the king's men were focused on orders to increase the security around the city walls, in case perhaps the messenger was intended only as a ruse and a distraction and some kind of frontal attack was actually planned. Wayland's first action was to check that Carter was still billeted in the same place. A quick glimpse through the open door as Wayland strode by the building told him that the man was still poorly but probably on the mend. Another few days and maybe he would be out.

There was still a lot of noise coming from the direction of the city walls, so he decided he would risk the walk to Alice's house. He was pleased when he reached her street to see that the repairs to her door had held. He hesitated a moment, then knocked.

'Who is it?' Her voice came through the closed door. She sounded cautious but not, he thought, fearful.

''Tis I, Wayland, the smith.' he said. The door opened, and she beckoned him in.

'Thank you kindly, Blacksmith Wayland, for the food.'

'I've more,' he said, fumbling for the package he'd concealed in his shirt, 'but it's not much.' He looked at her, but her gaze was only for the food. She tore open the leaves he'd wrapped the meat. He noticed, as she ate, that her teeth were white and strong.

'The leaves,' she said, 'what are they?'

'Dandelion. They would have a yellow flower. Doubtless you will have seen them in meadows, in happier days. You can eat them.'

She did so quickly then fetched a jug of small beer and they both drank a little. 'I must thank you again,' she said, 'but I hope you don't...'

'I'm not looking for anything more.' he said, quickly, but even as he said it he knew he looked directly at her in a way that he'd not be looking at a man. He turned away. 'I'd best be off then.' he said, not moving.

There was a pause as neither of them made a move nor spoke. Then Wayland moved towards the door. She stepped quickly into his path, kissed him briefly on the lips – and pushed him gently out.

'I'm my own man in life,' he said, 'I'm not tied to any master. But right now, though, I am a tied man in some respects, while this siege lasts. Most times I can't come and go as I please. And that bothers me, especially now because, you see, I can't promise to return on any one specific day.'

'The smithy,' she said, 'you say I can find you there?'

'Yes, it's the same smithy as the town smith had.' he said and went.

That night was the first night Wayland had slept through without waking from his nightmares with a jolt and in a sweat. He thought it odd because God knew that with no sign of the siege breaking his situation was desperate and getting worse. And he felt that he was no closer yet to achieving any revenge for Rebecca.

24.

Four days later Alice did turn up at the smithy. Wayland had sent a couple more small wraps of food since he'd spoken with her at her house and his first thought was that she'd come to thank him. He was pleased that she'd made the effort.

'I've tried a couple of times to see you,' she said, 'but your man here –' she pointed at the officer slouched, listless, picking at his boots by the door, 'stopped me. But then the baker told me he's eased up a little.'

'He's no man of mine,' Wayland replied and then, more quietly and indicating the officer, 'he's Sir Charles Lucas's man.'

'They're confining you for hitting an officer? I'm sorry,' she said, then, quickly, also in a lower voice, 'I mean, you know, I'm not sorry you hit him, though.'

Wayland turned to look at his guard. The man still

seemed uninterested but Wayland never did like the thought of others overhearing his personal conversations. 'No, it's not quite like that. But to explain... well, there is a room upstairs,' he said, 'now don't misunderstand me. What I mean is, it's best for us to talk freely without Sir Charles and all knowing our business.'

Alice glanced down at the floor then turned to face him directly. 'I believe you,' she said, 'and I believe I can trust you.'

He climbed ahead of her, up the few steps into the low-ceiling loft room that served as the sleeping area for himself and sometimes the boy. Once she was in, he pulled close the hinge-less door and plumped up the folded bedding to form a rough seat. He explained about the guard and the reason for it. They talked for near on an hour, awkwardly at first but very soon more confidently. They told each other the circumstances that had brought them to this present day. Alice asked few questions, but those she did ask showed she understood and felt his pain. Wayland had never opened up like this before to anyone since Rebecca's death. For his part, he began to understand the kind of difficulties she'd experienced, living alone, without a man since her husband's death, always needing to be suspicious of men, struggling to bring in enough income from weaving, competing against men for Flemish custom for her finished goods. She told Wayland how she weaved 'bays' which were, she explained, a sort of woollen cloth. Together with other weavers in Colchester she was preparing to lobby Lucas to seek his consent for their trade to continue despite the siege, but she held out little hope of success.

Neither of them was over talkative by nature and after their unexpected opening up to each other they abruptly fell silent. Wayland studied the door, as though expecting someone to burst in at any moment even though he knew that Jonathan was busy with the horses and no one else should be likely to bother them.

'Well,' said Alice. Wayland turned to her, worried that she was going to leave. But she looked directly at him, moving a little closer. That was all it took. He knew what he wanted and more importantly to him in that moment, he knew that she wanted it too. Their kiss was long and slow. She pushed away the bedding and pulled him back onto the straw pallet and they kissed again.

'Are you certain?' he asked, 'What if…'

'The way this siege is going, we may have no what ifs.' she said simply. Neither of them said a word more. Their love-making was slow and gentle. Both he and she needed something utterly different from the harsh reality that had immersed them for weeks now. To Wayland at least, though, it didn't seem any the less intense.

Later, when they were quiet and rational thought was beginning to come back to Wayland, he noticed that the rain-laden air had added to the sweat from their exertions. Rivulets were trickling down through the dark, wiry hairs on his chest. Alice was also coming to and she instinctively drew back from the damp heat of his body. They lay together a while on the now moist straw. Wayland looked over her skinny body, only now noticing the differences from Rebecca's plump frame. At first her whole body was moving a little, her panting in the process of subsiding but soon she lay still. It was then that a slight movement in her hair caught his attention. He watched as first one, and then a second louse emerged onto her neckline. She opened an eye and caught him staring.

'I was more than skin and bones before this siege,' she said, pulling her skirts up to cover her body.

He stood up, slowly so as not to alarm her. 'It's not that, I mean, it's just that I'm hot.' he said. Moving to the corner of the room he tipped half a bucket of tepid water over his head. He rubbed his hair vigorously before pouring the remaining water onto his chest and using a handful of straw to take away most of the water. 'Stay here,' he said, 'I'll be gone only a minute.' Before she could object he was gone. True to his word, though, he came back quickly and sat down beside her. 'Now,' he said, 'don't take this wrong. I've brought you a posy.'

She stared at the twigs he was holding. They looked a little spiky, but she saw that he had tied them roughly together. She raised an eyebrow in question.

'Rosemary,' he said, 'and, ah, two other herbs. They make life difficult for lice. They don't solve the problem altogether, but they do help keep the critters at bay. My wife had a great knowledge of herbs and I still remember some of it.' He lifted her long dark hair away and tucked the sprigs behind her ear.

'Oh,' she replied, blushing, and then she said, 'thanks.'

Wayland stroked her hair back over her ear. He didn't know what to say next.

'How long ago did your wife die?' she asked.

'She died over one year back,' he said.

They lay together a while but both were tensed up now. He wondered if his clumsy gesture and the mention of his wife had come between them but also both of them knew that this time in the little upstairs room was likely to be cut short at any moment by a shout for him or for her. It came soon enough.

'Smith! You're wanted. Now.'

He pulled on his jerkin and she adjusted her petticoats and skirts. She looked into his eyes when he bent to kiss her, and she reached for the herbs and rolled them into the back of her bonnet before tying it firmly by its ribbons. 'Wait,' he said, his back turned as he pulled up his breeches, 'when can I – I mean when can we...'

But she was already gone. Instead he saw two of the King's men, standing by his furnace, smirking, as he tucked his shirt back into his breeches.

25.

The other consequence of the attack on Alice was that clearly it changed the position with regard to Carter. At first Wayland did worry that, despite his previous, confident dismissal of such a possibility, Carter might have reported the attack on him and it played on his mind that unpleasant consequences would follow. A few more days passed uneventfully though, and the uneasy feeling began to leave him. Instead, he and Alun discussed again and again their hoped–for encounter with Carter and what it might mean in terms of opportunities to question the man further. One morning they were sorting through the charcoal stores, setting to one side the big lumps needed for the smithy furnace and to the other side the smaller pieces more suited for the bakery oven. Wayland suddenly picked up the bellows and threw them into the far corner of the smithy.

'When?' he shouted, 'When will God grant me the truth? Will we never get any further with our search? Can we never find justice for the boy's death? Or for Rebecca's death? We will likely perish in this Godforsaken town, murdered by one side or the other. Or starve to death. All for no reason.'

They had no time for further discussion, though. There was a familiar shout of 'Smith! You're wanted. Now.'

They heard the sound of heavy boots coming towards them. Only the King's officers still had their proper boots whole and intact. Wayland recognized the men who crashed into the smithy as two of Lucas's most trusted officers. 'You,' said the first officer, 'Sir Charles Lucas has ordered you to be confined.'

'Confined?' said Wayland, suddenly calm, to his own surprise, 'Are we not all confined, here in this town?'

'None of your insolence.' said the officer and he leant forward and slapped Wayland across the face with a mesh–gloved hand. The blow left track marks over Wayland's face where the metal had scraped his skin away. The other officer reached behind Wayland, jerking him arm up until it locked. Wayland said nothing, but his face turned white, making a greater contrast with the vivid red welts.

'Get him out of here!' barked the first man.

'Sirs,' Alun asked softly, 'where are you taking him?'

'That is none of your business. Unless you would like to join him.'

The second officer, pushing Wayland in front of him, went to follow his comrade but paused at the door. 'Lockup,' he mouthed to Alun, 'beside Head Gate.'

Wayland was taken, half dragged, half pushed, across part of the town and pushed into a dingy, windowless room. From the pungent smell of horse urine he realised it must have been a stable until recently. The iron bars across the one window were now planked over with wood on the outside, rendering the room so dark that he could at first see nothing. The officers had flung him in none too gently and he stumbled over the wet, stinking straw. 'Wait,' he shouted, 'who accuses me and what am I accused of?'

'This is a time of war. You needn't expect some orderly form of justice.' was all the answer he got. That and a guffaw.

'I should still be told!' he said.

There was no further reply as the door crashed shut. Feeling with his hands, he found a relatively dry spot of straw and sat down. He guessed Carter had complained after all. So the crucial thing now was to try to work out what the man would have said, in order to counter the accusations, whatever they were. His eyes gradually adjusted to the meagre light and he could make out a pail in one corner and two bowls in another. The first bowl had black stains but nothing else. The second had some yellowish water. He had to smell it closely to make sure it was water and not urine.

Nothing else happened that day. No one brought food or even water. He passed a restless night, uncomfortable on the scratchy straw, his mind churning with the possible punishments they might choose to inflict on him. The second day, though, some bread and clean water was brought in. Soon after that Wayland heard more footsteps and then some kind of struggle or kerfuffle outside and it seemed to him as though a man – or men – were being pushed into a room next to his. The only words he could readily understand were those spoken in an exaggerated, polite tone by an officer: 'I am so sorry. But since your side doesn't believe in royalty, we shall not treat you as such,' and then in a normal voice, 'you're going to have to like it or lump it with the common prisoners.'

That door clanked shut and he heard someone fall on to the straw. There was a further jangling of keys and the door to his own cell flew open. A man was thrust into the room. The door crashed shut again. Wayland could just make out through the gloom some tatters of a uniform. A closer look revealed the once plain cut of the coat and that told him that this man was from the Parliamentary side too. Wayland himself had been a pikeman in the earlier war, before the army had introduced proper uniforms but he knew enough about developments in the new "Model" army to hazard a guess that this man was a musketeer. He was wary of talking to him, lest the secret of his own military past should come out. He also suspected that he guards would likely be on the lookout to ingratiate themselves with the King's officers by relaying back whatever their prisoners said that could be incriminating.

Two more days passed. Wayland and his fellow prisoner had exchanged some few words about necessities – necessities that were limited in their bare lodgings to food, water and the shared use of the bucket for bodily waste. Wayland was still cautious in his approach to the other man and it seemed such instinctive reticence was mutual. They were both, however, extremely bored. Wayland had found a bent horseshoe nail and he began scratching pictures on the wooden walls. At first he drew lakes of varying sizes and shapes. He tried to make the water look rough, as in his nightmares but after a while he found that etching smoother, more regular waves was somehow soothing and he filled a whole wall panel with them. It was the development of a large blister on his forefingers, rather than some spirit of generosity, that prompted him to offer the nail to the stranger. The man took it but simply stared at Wayland at first. He seemed to reflect a moment but then ventured a half–smile at his benefactor and began doodling on the wall on "his" side of their cell.

Next morning, when the sun had risen enough to bring their usual mean ration of light through the cracks in the wooden planks across the top half of the stable door, Wayland saw that the opposite wall was covered in scratched markings. Most of them seemed to be abstract designs, mere meanderings of the nail. Then Wayland noticed one quite different from the others. He stared. He moved in for a closer look. There could be no doubt. It was the sign of the Crossed Keys.

26.

ayland discounted all caution and spoke directly to his fellow prisoner. 'That sign,' he said, pointing to the Crossed Keys, 'why did you draw that? Do you understand its meaning?'

The other man looked up. 'No.' he replied and then appeared to regret having said anything.

'Look,' said Wayland, 'I'll be honest with you. I'm not some common prisoner and I'm no Royalist spy either. I'm just caught up in this siege because the King's men forced me along. In fact, if I had to choose, I should probably favour the Parliamentary side.'

The man said nothing.

'But anyhow, we need not speak of things of one side or the other. My interest is only in your drawing. For I have seen it before and I have a need to know more.'

'What does it signify then?'

'A wise woman explained it to me,' said Wayland, choosing to avoid mention of the magistrate to a prisoner. He went on to recount the explanation of the Crossed Keys cross as it had been told to him. When he'd finished, the man sat back, a little less tense than before and Wayland guessed he'd passed some kind of test. 'I'm Matthew,' he said, 'the King's men caught me right by the Gate when they sallied out. At first they treated me well enough, trying to trap me into informing stuff I didn't know anyway. Then they beat me, but they eventually found it didn't improve my knowledge any. Now they've slung me in here, I guess they've given up. My big hope is that Fairfax, my general, will agree to exchange one of theirs for me.'

Wayland gave his usual short speech, introducing himself as a blacksmith and added some words of encouragement on the idea of a prisoner exchange. They chatted a while about the madness of war amongst people of the same country. 'And the same God.' Matthew added, leading Wayland to fear a lecture along biblical lines. Matthew may have guessed his thoughts for he suddenly changed tone. 'But you were asking about my scratching on the wall,' he said, 'and I confess it's an image that has played on my mind too.'

'Why so? Is it something that is commonplace among you in Fairfax's army? Is it some comment on Papists?'

'No. 'Tis not at all commonplace, thank the Lord. One of our men – but maybe I should not say more.' He paused and Wayland allowed the silence to hang there a while, being careful to shield the intensity of his need to know. He realised from his words that Matthew was a man of some learning. Wayland supposed that such men were likely more easily offended. He resolved to deal carefully in speaking with him. He waited.

'But what hurt could it do in here?' Matthew finally continued. 'One of our men has, to my way of thinking you understand, turned from the true teachings of our Lord and is headed for eternal damnation. The Lord must catch him, for I fear our men will not.'

'Why not?'

'All his sins are hidden.'

'Hidden? Yet you know of them?'

'Hidden from sight or hidden in plain sight, under the cover of war.'

'These sins – are they crimes? For it has not escaped me that both sides in this war claim to have our Lord God on their side. Is it excesses you mean?'

'Excesses, yes, and abominable deeds.'

'But where does this Crossed Keys sign fit in?' Wayland asked, his heart quickening as he began to suspect he knew the answer.

'He has taken against all of womankind it appears to me. It seems, well, that he cannot restrict his killings to the legitimate and inevitable deaths of war. Atrocities do happen in war, this I know to be too true. But I'm not speaking of deaths in the battle heat. He kills when he can. He likes to kill slowly. And he cuts… he cuts the sign in their bodies.'

'Alive or dead?' Wayland asked.

'Yes.'

'Yes? Which? Alive or dead?'

Matthew swallowed hard. 'It makes no difference to him, so far as I can tell. The thing with him is that he must do it. If he cannot do it then and there, after the kill, he must return and do it.'

'Does no one stop him?'

'After the massacre of women at Naseby, there was some talk of action against those who committed the worst of the carnage, but the war moved on, with Prince Rupert attacking Leicester and the like. And besides, this man I'm speaking of and some others simply disappeared around then.'

Wayland could continue no longer in his role of impassive curiosity. 'Who is this man though?' he burst out.

'Of what importance is his name? Surely what he is and why he is so readily capable of such unearthly cruelty is more to know?'

'True indeed,' replied Wayland, struggling to contain his impatience, 'but have you any answer to those questions?'

'Well, no, not I. But some have tried to figure the answer and some have even asked him.'

'To what effect?'

'He does confess himself a convert and I have noticed that converts often turn to more extremes that those persons who converted them.'

'That is true. I have seen it too. But in this case he converted from what and to what?'

Matthew fidgeted with some strands of straw. 'He grew up – as many of us did – with the old Catholic beliefs. I'm not saying I have those beliefs now, mind...' Wayland nodded to show that he took no especial interest in Catholic tendencies. Matthew continued.

'Some said he turned away from that when the village priest ruined his young sister with a child. But in all honesty I do not know. I know only that his belief now, if belief is the right word, is severe in the extreme.'

There was no opportunity for further discussion. They heard the guards approaching. Keys jangled, the door was thrust open and a shaft of light blinded both men temporarily.

'Your lucky day.' said one of the guards.

'Yes,' added the other, 'but do we bring good luck or bad?'

27.

The guards, it turned out, had been sent to haul Matthew away. Wayland hoped for Matthew's sake that it was for some exchange of prisoners. He found though that he did not really miss his erstwhile companion, preferring to stay alone with his thoughts.

He had plenty of time for that, as it turned out. Days and days of it passed – maybe weeks, he lost count – until one day the same guards returned. 'Now it's your turn,' said one, his voice grim.

Wayland decided not to give him the satisfaction of a reply. They pulled him upright by the arms, marched him, squeezed tight between them, back to the smithy and hurled him down on to the stone floor. 'Get up and get ready.'

'Get ready for what?' he asked, but the soldiers were gone. Alun was there, though, tending to the furnace. He seemed unsurprised at Wayland's reappearance. He went to pull him up, but Wayland shrugged him off and stood up, patting down his rumpled jerkin.

'It seems there's a parley on tonight,' the guard continued, 'and Sir Charles wants a proper supper laid on.'

'I'm no cook,' Wayland said, 'you have the wrong man.'

'And I'm no wizard,' said Alun, 'what could I cook them? The townsfolk are eating dogs. The lucky ones anyway. I've seen some serving up rat.'

'And I've no time for wit,' replied the officer, 'when there are orders to follow. You are to slaughter a horse for us.'

Wayland realised the man was serious. A horse. Things had become that desperate while he was in prison. Immediately he feared for his own horses. Of course, they would be at greatest risk since they didn't even belong to any soldier. They would hold no value to the King's men. Horror-struck, he stared at the officers.

'Get to it, then, man,' said officer.

'Tell him the rest,' said the other officer, 'about the selecting.'

'Sir Charles says to...' he paused, searching for the right word, 'to *emphasise* to you that he doesn't want some tough old nag that's been eating the thatch off roofs...' he said.

'He says there'll be a time for that if reinforcements don't get here soon.' added the second officer, keen to say something.

'Do a smith and a baker ...' the first soldier almost spat the words out, 'need to know that? No they do not.' He turned back to Wayland. 'You're the horse expert. You're

158

to choose one, maybe one that's got some problem but still got some flesh on it. Here's Sir Charles Lucas's authority and seal. Choose the horse, show its owner the seal and kill it near the kitchens.'

'How? asked Alun, 'How is he to kill it? Must he wrestle it with his bare hands?"

'A knife.' was the reply.

Wayland thought quickly. 'Killing a horse with a knife we'll lose too much blood,' he said, 'they're big beasts. And… well, happen the blood will be needed for sauce and suchlike.'

The guard thought for a moment. 'Can you fire a musket?'

'No, sir.' Wayland lied.

'You can't give him a musket, he's not one of us, he's no King's man.' objected the other officer.

'Don't be an idiot,' came the reply, 'we're all stuck here. No one can get away. There are four thousand of us and only one of him and he's got nowhere to go.' He showed Wayland how to load the gun and Wayland tried to look as if he was learning.

'Ammunition is in limited supply – obviously,' said the officer, 'or I'd shoot a horse myself. We need you to pick the right one and we need you to know which part of the animal to shoot. I'm giving you just the one shot.' And with that, he turned to leave. The other officer barred his way.

'The other thing,' he said, looking at Wayland and reaching into a large bag, 'is that as we've just told you, ammunition is running low. We need more. We've gotten hold of these…' He pulled out a collection of musket balls and laid them on the flat of the anvil. Wayland spotted straightaway that they were Parliamentary supply balls – and therefore just that little bit too large to fit the weapons that most of the King's men carried. He guessed what was coming but he said nothing. 'No doubt you've got some equipment to file these down to size,' said the officer.

'Aye, happen,' said Wayland 'but I'll have to heat them up first...'

'Don't bore us with the detail, man. Just get it done.' Both officers made off towards the door. The second officer couldn't resist a parting joke. 'Go easy heating them up!' he suggested, 'Or you'll be firing bits of yourself at the enemy!'

Wayland clenched and unclenched his fists quickly in exasperation. 'When?' he called, 'When do you need them?'

'Tues...' the second officer began to reply, but he stopped when the other one grabbed his arm.

'Just get them ready by tomorrow.' he said and at last they were gone.

'Sounds like a sally out to attack is on the cards,' said Alun.

'Aye, and they good as told us when,' said Wayland, 'mind, who could we tell? Even if we wanted to. Better get on with it all, I suppose.'

* * *

Filing down the ammunition would be a fiddly but simple enough task for Wayland and he made a start by picking out the tools for that job first, to give himself time to think about the bigger task. He'd killed horses before but only as acts of mercy, finishing off injured mounts after battle. So he was reasonably confident that he could do it with minimum stress to the horse – and with just the one bullet. But it went against his conscience to kill an uninjured horse. He supposed he'd do it, of course, if he were starving. But while he and Alun had been short of food for days now, he didn't reckon they were starving – yet. Besides, he had no illusions that he or Alun would get any share in the meat from this horse. And his assessment of the King's men was that they simply weren't used to light rations. Nevertheless, this was clearly a case – as it was more generally, he supposed – of follow the order or risk some severe punishment, perhaps even his own summary execution.

Wayland ran through in his mind the town's horses that he'd seen and could remember. He tried to rank them in order of suitability. He soon realized that wasn't working and so he set out to walk round the various make-do stables that had been set up around the town. He cast a quick eye first over the cavalry horses, noting that while all of them had rather more rib showing than was healthy, none of them would fit the bill of 'having some problem' and anyway he very much doubted that Sir Charles would want one of his own horses killed however big a feast it might provide. He walked on towards the regular stables. These were owned by Colchester's main provider of horses for hire, but all horses in Colchester had now been formally requisitioned by Sir Charles Lucas on behalf of the King and by decree. In fact, thought Wayland, in practice every animal – and indeed every soul – in the town was now subject to Royalist command and whim, with or without the formalities. So original ownership need be no obstacle to Wayland's choice. Nevertheless, he knew he'd be loath to take away some poor widow's only horse, if there was any likelihood she'd otherwise get it back some day. So he passed by a couple of nags tethered on the small patch of common land. He found a couple of armed guards at the main stables and explained his mission, showing them the sealed pass signed by Sir Charles. The manservant left in charge of the stables stood by, wary, at the entrance. Wayland's two guards chose to stay there too, all preferring to leave him to his grim task.

Wayland walked past the fitter horses, those still in individual stalls, until he came to a wide open barn space where the weaker horses had been quartered. They formed a loose circle. Some were standing; some were lying down. He placed the musket on top of a pile of leather buckets. Two of the horses, hearing the once familiar noise of a man touching a bucket handle, looked up in hope but the rest remained listless, heads down. Wayland approached one that was lying down, eyes half closed. When it stayed down, acknowledging him only with a brief flicker of the ears, he knew for sure that it was pretty weak. He noted some hoof-shaped wounds on its hindquarters. Bullied, he thought, and denied what little food there was by the other horses. He reckoned it didn't have much longer to live. Still, he needed to be sure that it wasn't sick of some infectious disease. He knew his own life would not be worth a farthing if he poisoned half of the King's officers. He pulled up its eyelids and looked closely at its eyes. He checked the nose and ran his hand gently over its flanks. 'You'll do, old boy.' he whispered.

Wayland reached out a small bag from inside his jerkin and pulled out a few sprigs of sage. He rubbed some over the barrel of the musket and pressed the rest to the horse's muzzle. Its dry lips slowly took in the crumbled leaves. The horse closed its eyes as the taste reached its brain. Wayland slowly raised the musket and lined it up. He moved it cautiously forward until it was almost, but not quite, touching the animal's head. He braced his own body for the kickback – and fired. There followed a cacophony of horse noises as the stronger horses panicked. One of the guards cursed. At first Wayland could see nothing but once the smoke and stable–dust cleared, he saw that his aim had been true. The horse lay, flat out now, stone dead at his feet. There was very little blood. He set off back to the officers' quarters. He found the one who'd instructed him, playing some kind of betting game with his fellow officers. Wayland reported back that he'd carried out the order.

'Quickly done, I'll give you that,' said the officer, 'but where is it?'

'Aye. Well the carcass needs shifting quick too. I doubt it'll stay whole there for long before others will be feasting instead of your commander.' Wayland replied. The officer glared at him but got up quickly and left, shouting orders for the butcher to be found.

Wayland looked in on his own two horses back near the smithy. His grim work today had brought home to him all the more the threats to their lives – and to his own life and Jonathan's.

28.

Thomas Fairfax was Commander–in–Chief of the new Model Army and, more specifically, at this time General to the besieging Parliamentary army. Previously *Sir* Thomas Fairfax, he was now a Lord, following to his father's death only a few months back. He was known to many of his men, though, as 'Black Tom' as much for his demeanour as for his darkish complexion. He had the respect of all his men but not the affection of all of them. Most found him too intense and many, including some like Nehemiah, totally failed to understand his persistent struggle to impose on his men his high standards of behaviour and forbearance towards the enemy. For his part, Fairfax saw little reason to explain his philosophy for in his mind it was just that: an essential philosophy. Orders, on the other hand, were basic instructions and he expected his men to obey them without hesitating, faltering or questioning. Renowned as a military strategist, he was usually inclined to prefer planning his army's next move in great detail to picking over the past or dwelling on it.

He was sitting at this moment, however, at the little writing desk that he had brought with him in the baggage train. He was brooding. It was one of those days when his gout–plagued foot would swell up, sending arrows of pain up the leg and – it seemed to Fairfax – straight into his brain, scattering his orderly thoughts. It was at such times – and only such times – that the doubts were able to creep in, if only briefly. Today it seemed that all his mental diagrams of siege fortifications and possible points for penetrating the city walls were being ousted by fleeting images from three years earlier, Naseby. First came a flash of pride, remembering how his men had acclaimed his courage in personally capturing the enemy's colours. How closely he had worked with the great man himself, Cromwell, in implementing the pincer movement strategy that had won the day! But shame soon followed, like a familiar whisper in his ear.

'The women…'

The thoughts kept pressing their way into his mind however hard he tried to push them away

'The slaughter of the women. So many women.' He knew that the fact of their deaths and even the atrocities, the maiming, had not dented his reputation one little bit, where it counted, that is, with Parliament. His standing was still good with Cromwell and as for his men, while they never somehow seemed to warm to him, he knew they did admire him for his successes. More widely, from the little he'd heard, news of the slaughter had barely travelled. Those who had heard of it seemed to have accepted the notion that the women had been Irish and so, in their eyes, deserving of everything – anything – in revenge, as some kind of repayment for the massacre of Protestants in Ireland some years ago. Knowing all that, though, didn't help Fairfax. It rankled the smooth cover of his own view of himself as an honourable man. He needed to cling on to that image. The way to banish these troublesome concerns must be to try all the harder to live up to his image of himself. Honour and reputation were life's blood: to be honourable even in war, however trying the enemy was. And right now the enemy was indeed very trying.

He paced the floor, trying to summon up some thoughts of military strategy and tactics to eject the visions of the butchered women, the screaming, the mutilations. At last the beginnings of a plan came to him and the images of women disappeared again. He sat down and began to compose a message. One that would set out exactly how the besieged Royalist army must surrender. Now, since there was no hope of any relief forces arriving, the only foreseeable outcome was the complete defeat of the King's Men, one way or another. As Lucas would know – should know – there was no dishonour for a commander in surrendering under such bleak circumstances of siege. And he, Fairfax, would offer honourable terms – the most honourable, and yes, fair, terms.

Later, when his messenger had returned with the report that his offer of honourable surrender had been rejected out of hand, he fumed, alone in his room once more. How dare they reject it? Rightfully, in God's eyes now, all responsibility for the consequences, for the deaths and mayhem that would now – inevitably – end this siege must surely lie with those inside the city. So, on their heads must it be. They – Lucas, Lisle, Norwich, all of those in command – they would answer for it. Not Sir Thomas Fairfax.

The butchered women did not return this time. Their screams had finally fallen silent. Fairfax felt calm, clear-headed. He felt himself absolved.

29.

Alice had taken to visiting Wayland every few days since his release. On one such visit, he told her to bring a spare set of clothes. She looked at him, puzzled, but with the guard approaching she didn't question him. On the next occasion, after they had lain together in the little room, he took both sets of her clothes and went down into the smithy. Alice looked down through the open door into the smithy. She saw a large pan of water, the pan that he usually had ready for the hot irons his work involved, already set up by the furnace. He heated his largest iron until it was white hot and plunged the iron into the pan of water. There was a great hissing of steam and for a long while Alice couldn't see through the steam. When it finally cleared she saw him add some herbs and what looked like tobacco to the water. She nearly shouted out to Wayland when she saw him dunk her clothes into the mix. Instead, she stepped carefully down into the smithy.

Hearing her, Wayland looked up in surprise. She was wrapped in some of the sacking cloths from the bed.

'Nah,' he said, 'don't fret. We'll give them a few minutes in water, then I'll dry 'em for you. Won't take a minute in front of the furnace, you'll see.'

'But why?' she asked, 'I've not dirtied them yet.'

'It'll fix the little critters,' he said, 'they'll not bother you any more after this.'

'Thank you,' she said simply. She was quiet a moment. 'You're a very kind man. You obviously care, and you think about the details. But... I wonder...'

Wayland looked up. 'Wonder what?'

'Nothing. You'll likely be mad with me.'

'I should be mad with you? Me? No, of course I shall not. Tell it. Whatever it is, tell it to me.'

'All right, I will.' she said but still she hesitated.

'You have my word. I can't say fairer.' said Wayland.

'Well, you are being very thoughtful. Kind. I just wonder if, perhaps, sometimes you overlook the bigger things. Sometimes. But it's not really my business. I mean I don't know...'

'What bigger things? What don't you know? Tell me straight.'

'I mean Jonathan.' she said, patting his arm in expectation of rebuff.

'Jonathan? What about him? What's he got to do with it?'

'Well... he's just a boy, Wayland, a boy who's been hurt and hurt bad.'

Wayland stared at her.

Alice took a deep breath. 'He doesn't talk. I see that. But I think he might. If you encouraged him more. If you gave him a chance.'

'Of course I give him a chance. Do you think I haven't tried?' Wayland was nearly shouting now, but he just caught himself, remembering his promise, in time. He looked down at the floor.

'Think back to Rebecca,' said Alice, 'how was she with the boy?'

Wayland thought. Pictures came to his mind, fast and seeming so real: Rebecca hugging the boy, soothing the boy, listening attentively to his chatter, smiling, laughing.

'Now think of you and the boy,' said Alice, 'when he looks to you, your face is set, grim. You barely speak and when you do, it is to command. When you talk with Alun, even in front of the boy, it's mostly talk of revenge.'

Wayland looked at her. His mouth opened but no sound came out.

'But I am his father, I am not a mother to him,' he said, finally, 'and I do need revenge – that's very real. How then can I be otherwise?'

Jonathan had been out, helping the men of the town, under the direction of Lucas's men, in the daily work of repairing and bolstering the town's ramparts. They heard him arrive back now, with Alun. Wayland was muttered a curt goodbye to Alice. Jonathan stared at her then turned to Wayland, curiosity obvious in his face. As always, though, he said nothing. In his present mood this merely irritated Wayland further.

'Don't stare, boy! Get away with you. Go. Go and … and see to the horses.' Wayland said. and he shoved the boy away.

Alun took Jonathan's elbow and led him out of the smithy. When Wayland turned back, the doorway was empty. Alice had gone.

'Damn it!' Wayland kicked a broken pike head across the floor, 'Such a stupid boy.'

Alun walked back in. 'Easy, man, take it easy. Think of it from the boy's position. He'll be wondering whether, since you seem to have a new woman, if she'll be replacing his mother.'

Wayland opened his mouth to reply then closed it again. He sat down abruptly. He banged his fist on the rough table.

'Matter of fact,' said Alun, 'what is going on?'

Wayland was silent a moment. 'Questions, always questions, never answers.' he said finally.

'Maybe you if you talked to the boy more you'd both gain something.' said Alun.

'Oh. You as well? Well maybe if you minded your own matters…' Wayland stopped short, only to continue, 'I'm not one for fancy speeches, explaining this, reassuring that – besides, the boy needs to –'

'There,' interrupted Alun, 'you've said it yourself.'

'What?'

'Boy. He's still a child. A child who's lost his mother – and in such very violent circumstances from what you've told me. It's affected you bad enough… think what it's done to him.'

Wayland scowled, but Alun continued. 'Chasing revenge is one thing. But seeing only revenge and missing what's right in front of you is another.'

Alun paused to look at Wayland but all he got in reply was a grunt. 'I'm off, then,' he said, 'if you've nothing else to say.' With that, he left Wayland sitting there.

Wayland continued to sit there a long time. He knew he felt bad but he was unable to fully acknowledge, even to himself, that Alun had a point. He tried to steer his mind away in a different direction. He tried to concentrate on Alice in bed, how she'd looked without clothes but again and again it was those recent words of hers that came to mind and that just added to his uneasiness. He pushed away both paths of thought and set his hands to work with the metal, as was his wont, and his brain to brood again on thoughts of death – Rebecca's death, that young boy's death, how their killer should die in turn. All he needed was the chance to find him. Surely God owed him that. He, Wayland, could take care of the rest of it.

30.

Sir Charles Lucas had chosen to head for Colchester in the first place because it was his home town. His family estate, a large manor house, lay just south of Colchester's town wall, in the grounds of St John's, the crumbling and now disused Abbey. He had come seeking the supplies and security he expected his home to provide while he waited for reinforcements. Now, however, his home was beyond his reach and only a source of worry to him. With Colchester now fully under siege, Lucas was trapped, stuck inside the immediate town, reliant on just a small force of loyal men to protect his home beyond the city wall.

Granted, for now Sir Charles Lucas himself was quartered beyond the reach of his enemies but whenever there was a lull in the defensive and offensive actions of the Royalist force he commanded, he fretted about his home. It was to turn out that his fears were by no means unfounded. For while Sir Charles Lucas remained besieged in his quarters in Colchester, Fairfax's army, impatient and uncomfortable, were likewise forced to remain, restless, in their newly dug trenches outside the town, day after day and night after night, soaked through to the skin more often than not. With no near prospect of a call to arms, after the rain, boredom was their main enemy. When they weren't wringing out their clothing or bickering in irritation with their fellows they mostly turned to fantasies of warm beds and willing bed companions. And so, when a suggestion was made to sally out, there was no shortage of volunteers. Nehemiah was one of them. If only he had not gone, if only they had followed a different route, maybe things would have turned out differently. But then again, given so much misery and pent-up emotions, maybe not so very differently.

The force chosen for this expedition was not overly large. Many men were left behind, disappointed, but it was obvious that too large a party would be more easily spotted. Their leader for that night knew about the Lucas estate. His simple goal was to check out to what extent it might be guarded and to take it if possible. He knew that his commander's thinking was that it could prove a useful bargaining tool. However, once the little party reached St John's, they met with a fierce, if short, resistance. The Parliamentary side soon overcame the defenders but the men were resentful, disgruntled at the unexpectedly hard fight they'd had. Once inside, though, they found that everything was still ordered as a great house should be. They ran quickly through the empty halls and high-ceiled rooms, pausing just momentarily to marvel at the paintings and tapestries. They reached the kitchen, stopping briefly to smash open a few earthenware storage pots. They carried on to the wine stores: Lucas's prized wine collection stretched out before them. Faced with such large quantities of fine wine after so many privations, the men had little hesitation in opening some. Bottle tops were smashed and their contents poured down throats. Unused in recent weeks to alcohol, they soon felt its impact. And as most men know, wine generally calls up the urge for more wine.

Swaggering and laughing, bottles in hand, they moved further in through the Lucas properties and into the church of St Giles. The Lucas family had used the little church, set within the grounds, to house the tombs of their dead. When they reached these tombs, only two men had doubts and drew back. The rest pressed on. Inside, the dark mausoleum that might in different times have seemed oppressive and solemn simply struck the men as another dry place, a welcome relief from the rain and mud. 'I've heard,' said one man, 'that such folks as the Lucases – Knights, Lords and the like – they bury their dead in their finery, with jewels and all.'

'Well,' shouted another, 'I wager that you could be right. And I can think of one sure way to find out if that's so or not.' He climbed up on to the nearest structure and threw his weigh at its stone cross. There was a loud crack as the structure snapped at the base, its weakest point. With a shriek of triumph, the soldier hurled the cross down on to one of the tombs, smashing it open and sending dust and stone chips flying. Straightaway, hands rifled hungrily down through its contents but managed to seize only dry and crumbling bones. Most men were so drunk by now that it didn't take long before a childish throwing fight began. Bones and dust dirtied the air. Nehemiah kept well back from this play fight though. He could see some more tombs a little way off. He was one of the few in the group there who could read a little. He was also less drunk than most. He moved away from the melee and began reading the inscriptions.

'Hey now,' he called out, 'listen up: here there are two corpses only a little while buried. Women they are too, the writing on their tomb says: *Margaret Cavendish* and *Mary Cavendish*.' Nehemiah drew back, unnoticed, as men rushed to crowd around the tombs. Intoxicated and frenzied, they battered these tombs until they too were smashed. A couple of men with stout poles soon lifted off the shattered stone pieces. There was a sudden, brief silence as they inspected the corpses within. None of the men noticed any stench of decay – the air was already ripe with the smells of sodden clothes, sweat and wine. They crowded forward to look inside. The bodies they saw were still recognizably female. Their chests had caved in, but their faces were gaunt and tight. 'Well,' said one of the men, 'you said it right enough. These are women. Not the best looking I've ever seen though.'

'Don't they say beggars cannot choose?' laughed another and went to lift up the skirts of the corpse nearest to him. Somebody else went for the hair.

'Look,' yelled that one, 'feel it – the hair. It's still soft. So soft.'

This sent the rest of the men into a fever of grabbing. As soon as the first man had pulled a handful of the corpse's hair, everyone wanted some. Nehemiah sidled off back to the wine store and brought back more bottles. His action – and he knew it well – was like stoking a fire. There was no limit now to the craziness of this mob. They fastened bones and clumps of hair to their clothes. They roared, they laughed, they sang bawdy songs; they urinated into tombs. The desecration of the Lucas family mausoleum was total, utterly complete. Nehemiah smiled to himself. The extreme acts of his fellow soldiers pleased him. He conjured up a mental picture of the grief and helpless anger that Sir Charles would suffer when he heard about it. But still it occurred to him that this pleasure was not enough. He had – he realised it now – no physical arousal. The whole experience was too frenetic and too... shared. He knew for sure then how he far preferred to act alone and deliberately. And he preferred real blood and some pain to watch. A lot of pain. He needed that, and the need felt urgent.

31.

Over the next few days, Wayland and Alun took it in turns to pass by the building where Carter was recovering, to look in and to observe, unnoticed, the man's progress. They became convinced that he was much better. 'I reckon he's faking it now,' Alun said, 'yesterday I saw him walking, bending down, picking stuff up from the floor. The man was positively skipping – when he thought no–one was looking.'

'Wouldn't you?' asked Wayland, a sour look on his face, 'Wouldn't you play it up if you thought you could sit there, day after day, being fed the King's men's rations, not having to fight and not having to risk death.'

'And not having to build ramparts while dodging enemy fire or harvest parliamentary cannon balls in the night from the rubble they've made in the day,' said Alun, 'that's what they've got me doing, that's my lot now – forget that it's one I never signed up to. It makes work such as the kneading and stoking the ovens seem easy as making daisy chains.'

'Stop grumbling,' said Wayland, forgetting that he had begun it, 'and start thinking how we can get to him again.'

Chance was to deliver them a second opportunity to quiz Carter sooner than either of them expected. Wayland had just been paid for some delicate repairs to Sir Charles's own armour. Money in the besieged town was by now pretty much acknowledged by all to be next to useless and meat was mostly just a thought that filled men's minds. So this time his "pay" was in small sacks of flour. The flour was much greyer than it should be, and Wayland spotted some small movements in it that pointed to the presence of more than a few weevils. He doubted that Alice could make much of it as it stood so he'd decided to take it over to Alun to use for bread first.

Wayland was standing in the bakery, half hidden in the shadows behind the ovens, when Carter and another officer walked through the baker's hovel and into the bakery itself. 'Just pick up Sir Charles's order,' said the other officer to Carter, 'you can manage that on your own, now, can't you?'

Carter nodded.

'Only, the thing is, I've got to see a man about a dog.' the officer added, with a wink.

'We're not reduced to eating dogs, are we, while there are horses left?' asked Carter.

'*We're* not,' replied the officer, 'but the townsfolk are eating dogs, cats, rats, anything that moves. So, the way I see it, chances are that I can barter this dog for something that'll sell – when we get out of here. If the dog's still got some meat on it, that is. So I will see you back at our delightful lodgings. Don't let on to anyone, mind.' This last comment was spoken as he turned to leave.

'Baker!' shouted Carter, his voice taut with self-importance. Moving further into the room and seeing Alun, he said, 'Get me the usual order for Sir Charles –'

He stopped short as Wayland stepped out of the shadows and slammed shut the door, blocking his escape. 'Now then,' he began but got no further as Alun grasped his left arm while Wayland moved quickly to grab his jacket.

Without a word, Wayland wrenched Carter's right arm away from him and yanked it up behind his back until it was fixed in an arm lock. He was now able to control the man with one hand. With his free hand he flexed the long horse lead rope that he had slung over one shoulder. He threw it at Alun. 'Make a noose,' he said.

Alun stared at Wayland and fiddled a little with the rope. But he did twist it round until he had it where he wanted it. He fixed the slipknot and looked back at Wayland.

'Well?' Wayland asked. He turned to Carter, his gaze boring right through the man all the while to somewhere beyond him. He stroked Carter's neck. His calloused hands might have felt rough on Carter's skin, but the caressing action was gentle, almost erotic. Carter's eyes opened wider. Wayland nodded to Alun. Alun snapped the noose tight, relaxed it out into a loop again and repeated the snapping shut.

'Wait, you can't... Stop! I will tell you. But... but truth is, I only know that she was killed,' Carter said, 'that's all

I know. You have my word on it.' His words had come out fast, on top of each other but the mere act of replying seemed to lend him some temporary courage.

It exasperated Wayland though. 'You suggested rather more, somehow, back at that alehouse,' he said, 'and now you will tell me now all that you know. You may think you won't tell me. But you will.'

'I did not kill her, I swear.'

Wayland slapped him across the face. Blood dripped from his mouth, trailing a bright path down a face that was otherwise white, all colour leached from it.

'I didn't ask you that. I'm asking you now, do you know who *did* kill my wife?'

Alun could hear the danger in Wayland's sing–song tone. He really hoped Carter could hear it. But Carter said just 'No.'

'Liar.' Wayland slapped him again. He turned to Alun. 'Fasten the noose,' he said, 'and hang it over that bar.'

There was an iron bar, fixed into the ceiling for the purpose of holding pans. Alun hurled the rope over it and caught it by the noose. Wayland turned Carter's head to face the noose as Alun steadied the rope and fastened the other end to a hook on the wall. The low light from the bakery furnace caused an elongated shadow of the noose to fall across Alun and the wall. Carter turned to Alun. 'Your sister did love me,' he said, 'and for that you should stop him.'

'That will hardly get me on to your side, even if it were true,' said Alun, 'considering how you left her to die.'

'I did not. It wasn't like that. It was war, it was chaos.'

'And this is not telling me anything about Rebecca.' Wayland said, raising his voice.

'Think,' said Carter, 'think what the king's men will do to *you* if you kill me.'

Alun looked at Wayland and nodded very slightly. 'More to the point,' said Wayland, 'I do concede that killing you *so soon*, might get in the way of you telling me what I want to know.'

Alun let the noose drop. Wayland appeared to think a moment. 'Well,' he said drawing out his words, 'my experience tells me that fire seldom lies.' He reached for the leather bellows and pumped away until the fire came alive again. He picked an iron bar that lay amid the fire making tools and plunged it into the fire's white centre.

'Think on it. It wasn't me that killed her.' Carter was sobbing now.

'Give me a reason, then, to believe you.'

Carter shook, his lungs heaving. 'God's mercy.'

'Ah, mercy is it you want?' Wayland hissed. Carefully, almost tenderly, then, Wayland pulled the glowing iron, now white with heat and dripping molten globules, out of the fire. His eyes shone bright with purpose. He brought the iron to Carter's chest with one hand and ripped away at his shirt with the other. Small iron shards hissed down into the water.

A sudden rustling broke the spell. Wayland's son crept into the room. 'What are you doing, Father?'

Wayland paused. It took a moment before he realised what had happened. The boy had actually spoken.

'Jonathan,' said Wayland, 'do you know this man? From... from before the siege?'

The boy shook his head.

'You've never seen him ... near your mam? Or anywhere?'

Another shake of the head.

'That's not him?' Wayland asked again but he knew now that it was not.

Not him? Then who? Wayland felt his mind clouding with uncertainty. He wanted to quiz the boy further, but some instinct told him that now was not the right time. He turned to Alun.

'It's all right Jonathan,' Alun said, taking the lead, 'we're just talking to Mr Carter. He's going in a minute. Go check the horses and wait for us in the stables.'

The boy left Wayland stood a moment in silence before reaching again for the iron.

'All right, stop, I'll tell you what I know,' said Carter. 'but just so that we all understand, neither of you will talk about me to Sir Charles Lucas nor any of his men. And I'll not mention you. We shall never speak in this way again. Put the iron away.'

It was clear that Carter's confidence was returning but Wayland slid the iron back into the furnace anyway. Carter took a deep breath and drew his shirt closed again cross his chest, pushing the ends back under his belt. He turned to Alun. 'And you, you remember, the same goes for you. I've told you all I know about Agnes.'

Alun opened his mouth as if to speak, then closed it again.

'As for Rebecca, Wayland, you were mostly right when you guessed first time. I was drunk in that alehouse and I was playing you. All I do know is what I heard in another alehouse…' catching a look on Alun's face, he paused, then said 'yes, I do drink too much. You might drink too much if you'd seen the things I've seen.'

Alun looked down at the floor.

'What I heard,' Carter continued, 'and you may make of it what you will, what I heard was that your wife was killed twice. And the boy saw it. That's all I heard.' With that, Carter strode off towards the bakery doors. He paused again. 'I don't know why I'm saying this, after what you just threatened me with – but if the boy saw it, and that killer ever finds him again, he could be in danger.'

He left. Wayland and Alun looked at each other. 'Killed twice? What on God's earth does that mean?' Wayland asked.

'Maybe nothing,' said Alun, 'the man's a drunkard.'

Wayland thought a moment. 'Yes, there is that – though I doubt he's drunk right now.' he said.

32.

The more Wayland considered Carter's words, the more he fumed. 'What in hell's name did he mean?' he asked and kept repeating, 'Killed twice. It makes no sense!'

'No, that it doesn't,' said Alan, 'but before the boy gets back, *you* need to calm down.'

'Calm down! Calm down! But –'

'Think it through, man. You saw the boy reject the idea of Carter as the killer. Did you watch him closely? All right, he was not actually *talking*. But, first thing, he indicated clearly as saying that Carter's not the killer. So let us forget about him. My second point is: it seems certain, though, that he – Jonathan that is – did see what happened to Rebecca. And now listen to me. My next point is that I think he's close to breaking his silence. Happen he can tell you something useful and happen he will tell you. But

I tell you now, he'll stay clammed up if you go at him all fired up as you are.'

Wayland thumped his fist on to the wooden table.

'I mean it – calm your mood, your voice and the like.' Alun said, with more than a note of exasperation in his voice.

'Oh, God help me!' said Wayland. But he sat down.

Alun poured some cold water into a jar and handed it to Wayland. 'Settle yourself now,' he said. Wayland drank the water and they waited then, in silence, for Jonathan's return. Wayland had time to reflect on Alun's advice. Rebecca's words came back to him too, things she used to say about how sometimes he was too fierce, too abrupt with the boy. When Jonathan finally walked back in, Wayland took a deep breath and focused hard on keeping his voice steady and low.

'How were the horses?' he asked.

Jonathan stared at him and Wayland immediately feared that the boy would remain silent. 'The horses? Are they all right?' he asked again.

'Yours is quiet,' Jonathan said slowly, unused to speaking, 'but... but Runaway Tom has hurt his mouth, biting the door I reckon.' His words came quickly now. 'They've had no food a couple of days now. Father, we must do something.'

'Runaway Tom?' asked Alun, keen too to engage with the boy, to keep him talking.

'I named him after Fairfax,' the boy, 'because we'd all like Sir Thomas Fairfax to run away.'

Wayland was in no mood to talk about horses let alone to joke and he nearly snapped. But he remembered how attached the boy was to the runaway horse and he stopped himself. 'We'll think of something,' he said, 'and if I can sort the horses, keep 'em safe somehow, can you help me understand what happened to your mam?'

Jonathan looked up, meeting Wayland's gaze directly for the first time in a long while. 'It ... it hurts, father, it's difficult.'

'I know, son, but sometimes we have to do things that hurt.'

Jonathan walked past Wayland and sat with his back to his father. 'First we need to save Tom,' he said slowly.

'Can a horse be more important than your mam?' Wayland asked.

Jonathan stared back at him. 'No. But maybe we can still save the horses. It's too late for Mam. I was too late. That's my fault...' He ran out, sobbing.

Wayland got up to go after him but Alun stopped him. 'Leave him be for now. It's too much, too soon.'

Wayland sat down, his chest heaving. 'It's too much for me,' he said, 'this hell of not knowing.'

'Look, you still have a son. Don't be losing him while you go chasing shadows. Just give him a little time. Think it through.'

Wayland was not at all sure he could.

33.

*T*he act of shooting the horse had of course saddened Wayland but what worried him more was the realisation that this one horse would be just the beginning of a slaughter that would not end, unless the siege itself ended, until the last horse was killed and eaten. Excavations and fortifications were still being built outside, around the town walls – he could hear them night after night. So he saw no likelihood that Fairfax would back down now and simply depart from the Colchester. Nor did he see any sign that Lucas or any of the others would just capitulate. So his worries about his own horses intensified. He was not sentimental about animals, but he'd had his mare a long time, they understood each other, and she was valuable to him for his work. Then there was the matter of his son's deep attachment to the new horse – apparently now called Tom. He really thought there was a possibility that looking after Tom could help heal Jonathan. Try as he might, though, Wayland could think of no other plan for now for saving his horses except to keep as low a profile as possible. Escape seemed to be out of the question: some brave souls had left at night, passing through gaps in the fortifications but the obvious risk – that of being shot by either side – would be considerably increased for a party of three or even just the two of them on horseback.

Matters were taken out of Wayland's hands very soon. A call went out for all able–bodied men to take part in an expedition outside the city walls to raid for food supplies. Men experienced with animals were particularly sought after as the plan, it transpired, included the intention to bring back some cattle and sheep. Wayland was saddling up his mare preparatory to joining the line of men on horseback commandeered for the expedition when Jonathan ran into the stable area. Without even a glance at his father, he began to put a bridle on the other horse. Wayland thought of trying to stop the boy but he held back, reasoning that surely the officers in charge of the expedition would refuse to take such a young lad and so he need not risk his son's anger being directed against him.

Wayland and his son turned up at the king's men's meeting point, on horseback. The officer in charge walked swiftly along the line, giving men and horses only a cursory inspection. When he got to Jonathan, the officer asked his age. Jonathan said nothing. Wayland said the boy's age and explained that his son had a problem speaking.

The officer ignored Wayland but turned instead to Jonathan. 'I take it you can, however, hear? And follow orders?' he asked. Jonathan nodded and the officer continued along the line of men. 'You!' he shouted to the next man, 'You're slouching – are you sure you can ride?' A soldier nearby was sent to replace that man and the officer moved on.

It was a night raid and as they stole out beyond the town walls, the horses trod softly in the dark. The moon was nearly full but it gave but very little light through the thick cloud cover. Wayland felt a surge of the old familiar excitement in action, despite that fact that he knew this was not his fight and his role would be, in essence, to help those he still regarded overall as the enemy, the king's men. Jonathan rode close up behind him. It crossed Wayland's mind then that his son might be worried. He gestured to the boy, assuring him in a low voice that the horse would pick its own way over the uneven ground and suggesting that he should focus not on looking down but on listening out for cows or sheep.

At first they found nothing of interest. Once they were clear of the walls and out into the fields, horses and men slipped and slid in the mud, tripping occasionally over lumps of shelled masonry and even canon balls. Wayland was not the only man who found it difficult to refrain from cursing when his mount suddenly stumbled. Still, he hoped to himself, perhaps this expedition could play out to their favour. At last one of the men in front spotted a pair of horns in silhouette, jerking upwards. It turned out that they had located some twenty cattle. At this point, the expedition split into two. The mounted men were to go for the cattle and the foot soldiers were to go on to seek out sheep, as sheep were more used to being herded on foot.

The trick with the cattle was to surround them as quietly as possible and only then to begin to move them back towards the town walls, at walking pace. The cattle turned obediently at first.

Suddenly, one of the lead cattle, a nervous young steer, fell head first into a ditch. Instantly it set up a great bellowing. It seemed to Wayland that every other cow and steer joined in. The herd was panicking but not as one. Some darted off to the left, others to the right. The men soon abandoned all efforts to keep silent and added their shouts to the cacophony. Some started their mounts into a canter to head off particular steers making a break for it. Jonathan's horse, confused and likely unaccustomed to herding let alone shouting, reared up. Wayland saw Jonathan thrown off into a ditch. The boy let out a high-pitched scream. He turned his own mare immediately and went to help his son.

Checking him quickly over, he found to his relief that the boy was scratched and bruised but otherwise uninjured. At first he couldn't understand his son's continued distress but then he saw it. Runaway Tom was living up to his new name, high-tailing it off into the distance. In what he realised later was an act of extreme foolishness – seeking a kind of solidarity perhaps, Wayland turned to his own mare and whacked her rump with the flat of his hand. She leapt into a standing gallop – chasing after Runaway Tom.

The other men had resumed control over the cattle herd and were now some way off in the distance, headed slowly back towards the town walls. Wayland pulled Jonathan to him and together they turned back in the direction those herding the sheep had gone. It took them over an hour but they did eventually catch up with them. They managed too to infiltrate this group by grabbing hold of the horns of a runaway ram and forcing it back into the herd. Wayland was careful to make the boy stay clinging tight to those horns, ensuring him an alibi for the night's work.

It was only an hour or so before dawn when the sheep herding group and their captive sheep made it back in triumph through the town gates. Jonathan was still downcast, but Wayland whispered to him, assuring him that the Parliamentary army would likely find the horses and that in that way they would be fed and cared for – and not eaten. That was the best they could hope for them.

There was no sleep for Wayland or his son that night. They were obliged to help set up secure housing for the seized sheep and cattle, to make fencing to pen them in safely. The Parliamentary army bombardments started up again, regular as ever, just after dawn. They were particularly heavy that day and again all able–bodied men were called on this time to carry out urgent repairs to the town walls. This work continued on into the next night. So Wayland had to wait another whole day before an opportunity arose to speak privately with his own son. He joined the boy in the King's Men's stables. Jonathan was charged with mucking out the stalls though these days this was a somewhat easier task than before as even the cavalry horses were now fed so little that their droppings were far fewer. Father and son scraped away at the stable floor. Alun was leaning against the stable door, keeping a watch out for any soldiers.

Wayland tried again to reassure the boy about the fate of his beloved horse; he did his best, too, to sound hopeful that they could one day reclaim the horses, though privately he knew that to be next to impossible. To his relief, Jonathan did seem a little cheered just at the thought that the horses would at least be spared their imminent slaughter for the officers' pot. He thought to distract him by telling him something of how cavalry horses were trained. 'One of those,' here he pointed at the nearest cavalry horse, 'can leap many feet into the air bearing a fully armed man and lash out with his back feet to clear a way from enemy foot soldiers,' he explained. Jonathan listened but his face was unchanged. Wayland stopped talking and reached out an arm to his son, realising as he did that he hadn't embraced him since before he'd left for the army, years ago. Uneasy and unsure, he settled for a pat on Jonathan's shoulder.

'Jonathan, can you tell me now,' he said, looking him straight in the eye, 'about when your mam died?'

Jonathan shifted back against the doorframe. 'It's maybe best, easiest, if I don't look directly to you,' he said, looking away. Then he began.

'I will tell it – I will try to tell it – from the beginning.'

He told how he'd seen the water trial. This much Wayland had more or less pieced together most of it from the little snatches he'd managed to catch from the villagers. But he breathed in sharply when Jonathan mentioned finding his mother alive on in the scrubland around the pond. 'She was alive? She was definitely alive? No question of it?'

Jonathan nodded, his head tilted downwards.

'Then what?' Wayland asked, 'Why couldn't you save her?'

Jonathan's shoulders heaved and he began to sob. 'I tried, Father, God knows how I tried.'

Alun reached over the half–door and put a hand on the boy's shoulder. With his other hand he made a warning sign to Wayland to slow down, to take it easy.

Wayland realised that Alun was right. 'It's alright, lad,' his said, lowering his voice, trying to sound calm, 'just take your time, tell me what happened. Whatever it was, I'll not be angry. I promise you. But I do need to know.'

Alun scooped some water from the horse bucket and passed it to Jonathan. Wayland twisted his hands around each other, struggling to control his impatience. Jonathan took a deep breath, paused a minute and then began to speak again.

35.

1647

*J*onathan was squatting in the reeds at the pond's edge. A ragged shriek made him look back at the platform. The mob was focusing now on the next woman. This one was much older and the boy could hear her shouting back at them. Giving as good as she got, she cursed them all roundly. The boy clamped his mouth shut, to stop himself from speaking his prayers out loud. Still hidden by the scrubby undergrowth, he began to crawl to his left, getting closer to the edge of the pond. Soon he could even make out the second woman's face. It was old Mistress Bland. The men near his mother turned to look at this victim before reluctantly wading further into the pond to retrieve his mother's body. The boy screwed up his eyes, searching for signs of life in her. He could see none.

Carelessly, the men swung the body back and forth between them then with one big heave they let go, throwing her on to the pond's bank, into the tall reeds and bulrushes, just out of sight. Job done, they hurried back, eager to join the crowd in baiting the next woman.

The boy scuttled fast, around the pond, bending low to avoid being seen. Reaching his mother, he dragged her deeper into the reeds, away from the water. Instinctively, he turned her on to her side. Grey water gushed out of her mouth. He grasped her by the waist, pushed her head down lower and watched as more water dribbled out. 'Mam! Mam!' he said. His words came out hoarse. He was desperate to pitch it loud enough to rouse her – but not so loud as to reach the mob. Time seemed to him to pass without end, but it could only have been seconds before he saw her eyes flutter, then open. She coughed up more liquid. This time it was greenish and tinged with blood. But she was alive. The boy started on the knots, working them loose and throwing aside the ties. It was a struggle as the water had acted on the knots, tightening them.

'Mam,' he said, when she was finally free of both the ties and the sheet, 'Mam, we've got to get out of here. Now. Can you? Can you move? We have to get away before they come back for you. But we must keep down, we must crawl so they don't see us.'

Jonathan held tight to his mother, willing her to recover sufficiently that they could escape further, much further, away. He knew it would only be a matter of time before the mob came looking for her. She was still panting and gasping, unable, it seemed to him, to speak. He remembered then a time when he'd been helping out with a friend at lambing time and one of the lambs had run off, falling into that same village pond. His friend's father had simply waded in, picked up the lamb and turned it upside down, patting its back until water stopped falling from its mouth and it had started squealing again. He manoeuvered himself under Rebecca and half-lifted her up so that her head hung down over his shoulder. He thumped at her back from behind as best he could. It seemed to be working, after a fashion, as a green foam dripped down over him from her mouth, staining his jerkin. After a while, he propped her up against a tree trunk. 'Mam!' he said, 'Can you hear me?'

He thought her eyes may have flickered and her head nodded but he wasn't sure. It was then that he heard footsteps swishing through the reeds. He lowered Rebecca again so that she was lying down. 'Sssh!' He put a hand over her mouth.

'So here you are,' said a man's voice. Hands swept apart the reeds and a man strode through. He stood over Rebecca and Jonathan, his eyes glinting. 'Not quite dead,' he said, 'yet.'

Jonathan launched himself in front of Rebecca's prone body. 'Leave her alone. Haven't you... you animals done enough?'

'First off,' said the man, stepping forward, 'I'm not one of them. But that's not the point. The answer to your question, is no. Not at all.'

His reply puzzled Jonathan for a moment – until the man took out a small curved knife. He barely saw it move but he did see clearly the blood falling across his mother's face. A triangle of flesh fell down her cheek. He leapt forward to attack but the man flung him aside then bent down almost *casually to pick up a rock from among the exposed reeds. Jonathan saw the rock coming towards him. He even heard it hit. He fell back, blood streaming down from his head across one eye. With the other eye he saw the man kick out. The foot struck him first across his throat and he found his voice was gone. He couldn't speak, he couldn't scream. The next kick struck him in the stomach and a sharp, nauseous pain jerked Jonathan's whole body, doubling him up. His arms and feet seemed paralysed. He fell. With his one clear eye he watched, helpless, as the man wiped his knife on some leaves. Clean again, it shone briefly, reflecting the sun, before the man twirled it rapidly in the clay, making some kind of pattern. Then he saw the man crouched over Rebecca and starting to work the knife on her body, making the same patterns. Pain, horror and disbelief swept through Jonathan bringing total blackness with it. Briefly, though, before he lost all consciousness, he heard a manic, unholy sound. He realised it was laughter.*

35.

1648

*W*ork had dropped off for Wayland and as a consequence, of course, the number of small food packets he received in recompense had dwindled. Lucas, the other Royalist commanders and their officers were still known to have some reserves of basic supplies and certainly they still had wine – Wayland could hear them most nights, though the sounds of their conversations had been a deal more subdued these past few nights. Food was a constant worry for all of Colchester's other inhabitants though and as is so often the way, it was the ordinary townspeople who suffered the most. Every cat and every dog had been slaughtered and eaten. Rats and mice were scarce; trapping them had become an obsession for many. Fatballs made from tallow candles and flavoured with herbs were fast becoming standard fare.

Wayland's contact with anyone other than the military was constrained of course. The two guards watched over him most of the time and Alice's visits were few and usually unplanned. He did, of course, know that the food supplies were desperately short in the town. But even so he was taken aback, shocked by her appearance when she came that day after an absence of over ten days. The skin on her face was grey and drawn tight across her cheekbones. He thought it looked as though it might crackle and tear if he touched it. She was wrapped up in winter attire and, although it was still a grim wet summer, he knew it wasn't that cold that she should be shivering. He went to greet her but she simply stood, staring at him.

'We've decided,' she said, 'we're going out, whether Lucas will let us or no.'

'Out? What can you mean?'

'Through one of the gates, or one of those gaps in the ramparts, it matters not.'

'But why? And who is "we"?'

'Women, of course. They'd kill the men. But we shall go, as a mass. To beg for food.'

'From Fairfax?'

'Yes. He must know that our town is still for Parliament. We have no part in any king's fight. He must let us out of this Hell. Some bread, that's all we'll ask. For the children especially. So many... so many have died and die still for want of bread.'

Wayland thought a moment but he could not fault her logic. 'I knew it was bad but this is...' He was unable to find the words. 'The children, yes, I see. But it's too dangerous.'

'They will die here. What is more dangerous than that?'

'I… I don't want you to go.'

'I have to,' she said, her voice bitter, 'it's simple. Yes, we know the King's men have food. Maybe not much. Maybe not enough. But they still eat. And they refuse us any. Every scrap of food was taken from us and none has been given out for days now.'

Wayland knew then that she had no option but to make this attempt. He could see it was pointless to dissuade her whatever the danger was. His heart missed its dull beat as he wondered if he would ever see her again, if the Parliamentary forces did take in the women over on their side of the siege lines. He sensed, though, that it would be pointless to say anything of this. Instead, he hugged her close – and then she was gone.

Jonathan was lying, listless, propped up only by the doorframe. He looked at his father. Seeing such anguish, he raised himself up.

'I'll go with her,' he said. 'Children are going. I can look out for her.'

'You're a lad,' said Alice, 'so it won't work.'

'I'm small. I'll mix in. Father, let me do this. I've been powerless all through this siege. I can look out for her. I'm not as starved as they are. I'm stronger. I can help.'

Wayland felt torn in two. He saw the logic in his son's offer. He admired him for it. But then he would have both of them at risk.

Jonathan looked down, awaiting his father's word. He picked at his sleeve.

'Go then. But mind you keep your wits about you. And on no account bait the soldiers.'

Wayland walked out. He could not bear to think of it, let alone to say aught else. He slammed the door as he left the smithy.

Alice and Jonathan joined the gaggle of other women and children at the gate. They shuffled forward in sombre mood, out past the roughly hewn fortifications and towards the Parliamentary trenches. One of the women spoke: 'Get ready to make some noise,' she said, 'we will need to make our plea. We must be heard as women lest they fire on us.'

They stumbled on, a ragged line of women, clothed in flapping skirts now grossly oversized for their skeletal bodies.

* * *

Wayland walked towards the gate he knew the women had used. He had not gone far, though, when three soldiers stepped out to block his way.

'Go back, Smith,' said one, 'I doubt Sir Charles Lucas wants the enemy to see our side gawping at a gaggle of townswomen.'

Wayland felt the bile rise into his mouth, but he backed off without a word. That was when the noise started. It was far off but unmistakable. Women were howling and screaming. Men shouting. And then, after some minutes, came the sound of men laughing. A short silence followed. Then there was the clear sound of musket shots. Wayland wasn't able to count them but he guessed there were fewer than twenty. He knew that, unlike the Royalist's men, Fairfax would not be short of ammunition. There was nothing Wayland could do except pray that these were but warning shots.

His sense of frustration grew over the next few hours. The hours stretched into the night and still there was no news. Wayland couldn't understand it. If the women had been granted food and shelter, why had there been shots? If they had not, why were they not back within the fortifications? It made no sense.

* * *

Wayland's hours of waiting had turned into days before he heard anything of the women's return. This time, no one stopped him leaving the smithy and setting out for the gate. At first he was convinced the news was wrong. He could hear nothing. He expected to hear crying, talk – something. Then he saw them. There were fewer of them than had set out. There was something odd, too, about their clothing. Some of the women were half naked. Others had clothes in tatters. They staggered and stumbled, heads down, through the gate. Every child even was silent.

Wayland was about to set off towards them when he felt a hand on his shoulder. It was Alun.

'Think, man,' said Alun, 'you know, love is all very well but they need sustenance more than anyone has ever needed it.'

'But...' Wayland knew Alun was right but he had nothing, even back at the smithy, to give them.

'We can try Roland,' said Alun, 'if anyone has anything to eat – anyone that's not a King's man, that is, it'll be him. Bring them to the bakery. And fetch some blankets to cover Alice.'

Wayland stared at Alun, his brain slow to process his thoughts. He nodded.

'And don't go expected any account of what's happened until they have eaten,' Alun added.

Alun was proved right. Rowland managed to come up with some crusts of bread: scrapings from the baking pots and some tiny strips of what looked like it might be meat. There was water too. Alice and Jonathan tore into the food. Neither of them asked what it was. Wayland paced the small room while they ate. Alice spoke at last, 'They gave us nothing. They stoned us.'

'They shot at us. And...' Jonathan stopped short, looking at Alice for guidance.

'Their men came out from behind the fortifications. We thought... we thought they were coming to fetch us in. But oh, no. They came to humiliate us. They stripped many of the women. They got my shawl. Jonathan got me away then. And then... then they... well, they laughed at us.'

'Bastards.' said Alun, clenching his fists. 'And they call themselves the army with God on their side.'

'That's not all,' said Alice. 'When we got back, Lucas had barred the gate against us. Us, his own townspeople. We had no choice but to sleep in the ditches and trenches.'

No one said anything. Jonathan used his last pinch of bread to mop up the dampness left by the meat.

'Father,' he said, 'Father, you may not believe me. But I saw him. I swear it was him. He's one of Fairfax's men.'

'Him?' asked Wayland, but even as he asked the question he knew the answer. 'The man who killed your mother?'

'Yes. It was him. The missing ear. The voice. It was him. I know it was.'

36.

1648

'Why? Father, *why*?' Jonathan was shouting at Wayland now, 'I'm no child. I know men do kill and forever they will. But it's always for a reason – isn't it? For King or for Parliament or for robbery or...' He searched a moment for the right word, 'For lust and so on. But why my mam? Why did he kill her? And why did he have to cut her?'

Jonathan collapsed. Wayland and Alun sat speechless. Neither man had any idea what to say or what to do. So both stayed silent. Days had passed but still Jonathan asked the same questions, questions neither man could answer.

Alun was the first to hear the shouts outside. He went out into the street to investigate. Everyone was looking up into the sky. It took him a moment to realise what they were seeing: kites. Kites were flying overhead, their white tails streaming and dancing beneath them. It wasn't long before a couple of the King's men appeared with muskets. Their leader took aim, fired and missed. His men positioned their muskets. 'Idiots,' muttered Alun to himself, 'if they do hit it, they'll destroy any message.'

The futile shooting went on for some time before a sudden lull in the wind brought one of the kites down. It landed near Alun and he rushed to it.

'Stand back,' one of the soldiers bellowed, 'and step away or I'll shoot *you*.'

Alun jumped back – but not before he had seen something of the message attached to the kite. He could barely read but he could see that the full wording included some triumphant text and obscene mockery. He recognized the word "defeat" and he memorized another word in the message: Preston. Alun had no idea where Preston was but he did know that this must be big news. He extricated himself discreetly from the crowd and went to report back to Wayland. He spelt out the word in the earth.

'Preston,' said Wayland. 'must be a defeat for the King or they wouldn't be so keen to tell us.'

'Where's Preston?' Alun asked.

'That I don't know,' said Wayland, 'but it cannot be nearby or we would know it. Can you remember anything else?'

Alun thought hard. 'Apart from the cursing, there was this: H–O–M–A–T–O–N or something like that.'

'Hamilton? Hamilton is that name that the soldiers keep talking about. When they think no one is listening.

Some commander for King Charles he must be – and he is the very man Lucas has been expecting to bring the relief army here.'

'So, if this is true and not a ruse, that's their whole hope of winning a way out of this siege gone.'

'We shall know soon enough what Lucas and the others think. If there is truth in it, he must surely call for terms directly.'

Jonathan looked up now. 'You mean, they will surrender?'

'Aye, lad, though I doubt he'll call it that in any of his speeches. But yes, we're thinking negotiations will start. To get us out of here.' Alun said.

Wayland was still thinking. 'It's more than that, I reckon,' he said, 'with Colchester lost, the King's cause is surely done for forever. He has no other sizeable force, at least, none that I've ever heard about.'

News of the King's army's defeat at Preston soon travelled around Lucas's men and it was caused much agitation among them. It was received almost with indifference in the town at large, though. Those citizens who had survived so far – and a great many of course had not – were listless, weak from hunger and utterly disillusioned by so many previous rumours of some possible end to the siege. Wayland did, however, hear from one of the soldiers that Lord Norwich himself had formally set in train some actual negotiations for surrender and it was widely expected by the Royalist forces that his proposed terms would be agreed.

On the other side of the city defences, however, the Parliamentary commander, Fairfax, saw things very differently. It was true that Fairfax had long prided himself that he conducted war not just bravely but also efficiently and fairly. But it was also true that he relied heavily on the rules of war. Ordinarily, in the terms for surrender in wartime those rules, written or unwritten, would include standard, separate guarantees for commanders, officer, men and citizens. As Fairfax saw things, though, at least some of those commanding the Royalist side had breached other rules. And for him *those* rules were crucial ones that also governed how men *ought* to conduct themselves. Fairfax was focused especially on Lucas, the man he considered most personally involved in actively directing the enemy's military tactics. Only two years earlier, after an abortive rebellion that ended in defeat for him in Stow-on–the–Wold, Sir Charles Lucas had – as the very pre-condition for his release from captivity – then sworn a solemn oath never to bear arms against Parliament again.

The Royalist command as a whole was also gravely at fault, Fairfax considered, for having refused to yield the town as soon as all supplies had been so clearly cut off. That represented another violation of the usual laws and customs around war and siege. The siege had now lasted some eleven weeks: an unprecedented time in recent history. In short, Fairfax was of the firm belief that this prolongation of the siege was due solely to an utterly pointless stubbornness on the part of the Royalists. It had caused, there was no doubt about it, extreme and futile suffering within the town walls – but it had also brought a pointlessly long deployment of the Parliamentary army and many losses to his Fairfax's own troops. That he could not forgive.

And so it was that a cold, rule-based logic began its mix with a hot simmering desire Fairfax had for revenge. This was to have the same kind of effect as has oil when poured on fire. The whole of Colchester's besieged populace was soon to suffer these calamitous effects. Fairfax resolved first of all to add delay to the punishment he planned. He would need to make arrangements and to seek if possible some approval, formal or otherwise, from higher up. Thus, when the Royalist side's messenger duly arrived, breathless from his short but hurried journey from Colchester's town gate across to the Parliamentary fortifications, Fairfax made him wait a while. Opening the message back in his room, he saw that, as he had anticipated, Lord Norwich's proposed terms closely reflected those of a traditional standard surrender. He ordered the messenger to return empty-handed. He asked his manservant for a long drink for himself and he began to compose his own terms. Engrossed and enflamed as he wrote, he no longer noticed even the sharp pain of gout in his leg.

37.

That the kites and messengers represented an apparent signal of an end to the siege was greeted with such an apathy revealed to Wayland the extent of the townspeople's distress and disbelief. Those who were closest to starvation had long since let go of the hope of a quick end to the siege by way of the King's Men actually winning after some miraculous relief by Royalist reinforcements. It seemed much more likely that it would need a matter of time, time until Lucas, Lisle and their ilk had been reduced to the same state of hunger, misery and caring for nothing, as was the lot of the lowest orders. Owing to the Royalists' total control of the few remaining supplies, that had come close, but it had not quite happened yet. Instead it seemed to people that no matter how tough things became for ordinary folk, Lucas and Lisle and the other commanding gentry always had some reserve food stocks of their own. It was true that after the town's women had returned in such desperation from the enemy's front line, Lucas's men had released a small ration of the officer's grain for the townsfolk. But there had been nothing since. Many citizens, mostly women and children, had died of starvation and most of the remainder had now been driven to gnawing on tallow candles, on leather shoe uppers or even on bark. And so, while the people knew it to be true that the Parliamentary kites had skimmed over the fortifications, laden with written scraps of news of the complete destruction of the King's forces at Preston, who could tell for sure if such news was actually true? Lies, exaggeration and politics were weapons of war more often than not in these days of turmoil. So, most of the townspeople, and indeed Wayland himself, were not, for the most part, entertaining any thoughts of an imminent end to their hunger and misery. No one knew for sure if the Royalist commanders believed the news and, if they did, whether their reaction might yet be to continue to hold out against Fairfax. Sheer fatigue and the constant pains that hunger brings had driven out all but the very last vestiges of hope for most people.

Wayland himself had for some time now ceased to receive even the occasional meagre handout from Lucas's officers. Recently he and Alun would spend their evenings trying to extract the dried remnants of marrow from the few horse bones they could scavenge from odd corners of the main stables. On the occasions when he could smuggle a couple through to Alice they'd boil the bones up and drink the greasy water as a soup. It was true that Wayland had now heard it confirmed that negotiations were taking place and that Lord Norwich was proposing the terms under which he, Sir Charles Lucas, Sir George Lisle and Lord Capel would all sign to agree to a negotiated surrender. Unlike them, though, Wayland did suspect that Fairfax might reject those terms. And so, Wayland too remained listless in mood. Neither Alun nor Jonathan showed any energy either now.

During the previous weeks, Alun, mainly through his naturally cheery, jokey approach to things, had managed to befriend the soldier whose responsibility it still was to keep an eye on him. So on this particular morning in late August, the soldier brought Alun some flour. 'We're breaking out the very last of our supplies,' he told Alun, 'seeing as the siege must now end.'

'They've allowed you to bring that to us then, them in command, have they?'

'Not, ah, directly or as such,' said the soldier, looking away, 'but who is going to care when we're done here and out of this godforsaken town?'

'Well, my thanks to you,' said Alun, 'you have hope when no one else has then. But let's have a look at what you have there.'

'There's this too.' said the soldier, handing over a tiny packet.

'With this stuff as well, I reckon I can make a couple of bread cakes or at least something we can eat.' Alun said. He coaxed the remnants of the charcoal into to life, got some water and set to mixing. He picked up the mutton–fat candle he'd been forcing himself to gnaw on that morning and set it to melt for frying the mix. When it was done, the cakes looked more like greasy bricks than food, but the soldier happily took most of them away. Alun, Wayland and Jonathan feasted on the rest – for it did indeed seem a feast after so long with so little food. Wayland felt some little pleasure that at last some tiny amount of energy was coursing through his veins – but he could not know how crucial this little transaction with the soldier and this source of some energy would prove to be.

* * *

Lucas read Fairfax's curt response to his offer of terms of surrender. It was a counter offer – and Fairfax had made it clear indeed that this was to be the only offer – and that it was a non–negotiable offer. The terms of surrender were brutal. They stated that:

- Lords and Gentlemen were all prisoners of mercy, that is, their fate would be entirely up to their Parliamentary captors and would not be known beforehand.
- The common soldiers were to be disarmed and could be issued with passes to return to their homes only after they had sworn an oath not to take up arms against Parliament again.
- The town itself could be saved from destruction and pillage – but only if £14,000 was paid over in cash.

These terms represented more than a shock. To Lucas, it was beyond belief and it went against all military convention. Emotions surged and competed. First came fury. He had considered Fairfax to be an honourable opponent, hadn't he? Why would the accursed man do this? To be a prisoner of mercy was to give oneself up to the whims of the enemy. Fear came to his mind soon after, though, as he thought for the first time of the possibility of his own execution. Death in the heat of battle was one thing. A soldier didn't dwell on that. But the dishonour of – of what? He realized he didn't know. Would it be a hanging even – would they dare to do that? For a man of Lucas's rank that was unthinkable. And yet, with such open terms of surrender, what else could Fairfax be after? Next, his conscience threw a quick stab of guilt into the mix. He remembered quite sharply now his previous defeat. It had been during the earlier war against Parliament. He'd been Lord Astley's Lieutenant General of All the Horse throughout their battle and subsequent defeat at Stow-on-the-Wold. His disappointment at having to surrender in the market place there had been bitter. Being taken prisoner, though, had seemed more of a formality. That hadn't felt so final. He thought now of how lightly he had given his word, renouncing all intent to bear arms against Parliament ever again. He forced such thoughts away. Times had changed and surely serving his King – *the* King, the King by divine right – must come before any promise to men.

Later, having pushed away all such violent emotions, he found his brain, just recently so enflamed, now felt only deflated. A deep despondency was all that was left. With Norfolk, Capel and Lisle surrendering, Lucas had no other options anyway, even if he had been able to think of one. Slowly, silently, he added his signature and seal agreeing to the document of surrender. Without looking up, he pushed it into the hands of his messenger to take back to Lord Norfolk. So morose was he that at first he didn't even hear the commotion his own men made as they made ready to open the town gate and to lift away some of the many structures so hastily erected against the siege. It was only when the messenger hurtled back in and ran to the little window beyond his desk to watch the action that Lucas's mind snapped into its more customary, military mode. He strode over to the window and leaned out. 'You there! Halt!' he bellowed, 'I command you to take away only a few of our barriers. We must not give the Parliamentary forces any good chance of a stampede. Narrower gaps will promote in them a more orderly entrance.' He turned from the window. Lowering his voice, he added to no one in particular, 'And fewer odds on atrocities. Only God can help us now.'

* * *

Over on the Parliamentary side of the town walls a roar went up. The officers struggled to hold their men to some kind of disciplined line. The men had now forgotten all the waiting, the weeks spent lying in stinking muddy ditches, the cold, the boredom. Their minds filled now with the elation of victory, with speculation on possible plunder and above all with a strong need to be active. They wanted to rush into the town that had denied them entry for so long. More than one man harboured too some thoughts of a personal revenge, of payback for himself and his pains. But there was only one man whose thoughts were utterly dark. That man was Nehemiah.

38.

The main Parliamentary forces leading the advance had marched towards and then through Colchester's town gate in some semblance of order. By contrast, ragged streams of men now poured through the gaps in the fortifications made by the soldiers ahead of them. Immediately it became obvious that their progress was not fast enough for those behind and soon more structures were being smashed, broken and fired. Dense smoke began to add to an already dark sky and many officers lost sight, let alone control, of their men. The cacophony of noise became unbearable as these invaders roared, struck at any obstacles and fired their muskets randomly into the air. It was only a matter of minutes before the screams of women and children added to the raucous chaos. Wayland, watching from the empty hayloft atop of the stables, prayed that Alice remained safe, back in his room above the forge. He thought immediately of course of the boy and looked round to reassure him. But Jonathan was gone.

He scrambled down to floor level, yelling all the time for his son. He ran outside, asking people if they'd seen the boy, or indeed any boy. But no one heeded him. Every man seemed immersed in his own panic. Wayland circled the crossroads, straining his eyes down each street in turn, struggling to make sense of all the movement, to filter out from it any form that might be, that could at all possibly be Jonathan. Nothing. His chest heaving, he turned toward the bakery and ran on, hoping and praying that Jonathan would have had the sense to go to Alun.

* * *

Nehemiah and the soldiers he was with had now squeezed through the actual wall gates only to find that their way to the centre was partly blocked. Nehemiah stuck close to his group for now but kept his position towards the rear, letting the stronger ones among them struggle to move the fallen debris that narrowed their path and limited their passage through the abandoned siege blockades. When an especially large piece of fallen roofing blocked their way and looked likely to cause a significant delay, Nehemiah slipped aside into a narrow side street and picking on a small cottage, he set alight the few scrappy bits of thatch that had escaped being commandeered by the King's men for horse food. He waited only long enough to be certain that it had caught before he rejoined the others.

The orders given to the Parliamentary soldiers were to search for and take prisoner all those who were part of the King's command. The soldiers found it easiest in practice, of course, to assume for now that this would include any adult male who could not quickly and clearly prove himself to be *not* a part of that command. So the logic was that every house and building must be searched. Of course, if the searching revealed any valuables, these were not going to be ignored and, indeed, valuables were prominent in most men's thoughts – though not in Nehemiah's. It wasn't long before the little group stumbled across the row of houses that had been taken over during the siege to house the higher ranks of the King's cavalry. A rapid and vigorous search soon proved that the recent occupants had fled, leaving little behind. What they had left behind, though, included several pairs of boots. And after so many weeks spent lying in soggy ditches, no one in Nehemiah's group was going to overlook dry boots. There followed a melee of men trying on boots and swapping boots. Only Nehemiah held back. And as he loitered in the street, his eyes caught a movement. A boy. Alone. Slipping into a single storey building. Nehemiah set off after the boy. No one would notice his absence.

Meanwhile, back in his baker's quarters, Alun was scrabbling through a stack of iron pans, hoping to find one light enough to wield but heavy enough to serve as a crude weapon. He had his back to the door when Jonathan burst into the room. 'Mother Mary and Jesus!' said Alun, 'You startled me. I thought... I thought you were one of them.'

'One of Fairfax's men?' Jonathan asked, 'Well, you're not so very far wrong. They're coming all right. I came to warn you. Father was too busy watching them break through. But…but what are we to do? Will they believe us? That we are not for the King?'

'Steady on lad,' said Alun, 'seems you've a lot to say, now that you've learnt to talk again.' He made an effort to smile in reassurance.

'But you've not seen them,' the boy said, the words tumbling out fast again, 'I swear there's murder in their eyes and they're all fired up. Likely there'll be little time for explanations. We should hide.'

'Too late now,' said a voice so quiet and calm that Alun was not completely sure he'd actually heard it. For Jonathan, though, the voice was there – and he knew he'd heard it before. The man who stepped into the bakery was Nehemiah. 'Ah,' he said, 'so God has rightly given you to me this time.'

'You!' yelled Jonathan, 'You murdering bastard!' He launched himself toward Nehemiah.

Alun immediately took in that Nehemiah was holding a musket in one hand and had a large, curved knife at his belt. He acted quickly. Stepping between Jonathan and Nehemiah, he jumped forward. 'Whatever it is that you want with this boy, you'll answer to me first.' he said. Alun stared at Nehemiah, searching the man's face for clues to his motivation. Seizing his iron pan, he took another step towards Nehemiah. He grasped the boy's hand to hold him back.

'Let me go,' Jonathan screamed, 'you don't realise. He's the one who –'

This slight restraining action on Alun's part gave Nehemiah his chance. Without warning, without taking

220

his eyes off Jonathan, Nehemiah swung out his arm and struck Alun on the side of his head with the musket, knocking him out cold. Alun's body sagged and he collapsed in an untidy pile on the floor. Nehemiah stepped over him, towards Jonathan.

* * *

A group of Fairfax's men blocked Wayland's path to the bakery. Wayland stopped short then cursed himself for a fool. With a whole army of besiegers streaming into Colchester, how could he hope to protect his son against them all? Yes, he had some battle experience. And yes, he could articulate and reason where Jonathan could not. But to come out without any kind of weapon was nothing short of foolish. He retraced his steps, back to the stable. A quick search there revealed nothing of any use as a weapon. He ran on to his smithy.

Back inside the smithy, he sorted impatiently through the pile of ironwork stacked up against the far wall, picking up pieces then hurling them to one side. There were muskets that needed fixing – useless without ammunition or powder. He picked up one of the broken pikes. It was a weapon sure enough – but too obviously so if he were caught with it. He had no desire to be seized as a soldier before he could find Jonathan. He threw it down and moved over to his collection of tools. He picked one out: a heavy, long–handled branding iron. About a foot and a half long, it was heavy enough. It would do. If challenged, he could legitimately point to it as a tool of his trade. Assuming they did ask questions first, that is. He transferred it to his left hand and hurried back out.

*　*　*

'Let me go,' repeated Jonathan screamed, 'you're the one who –'

'Killed your mother.' The quiet, steady voice took over, finishing Jonathan's sentence, 'Yes I am that man. And I'll tell you something else. It pleased me some, doing it, watching her face when I cut –' he paused to study Jonathan's face as all colour drained from it. '– into her smooth, white breasts.' he continued.

Jonathan stood there, shaking, as shock, anger and fear all vied for control of his mind. Alun was still slumped next to the ovens, blood now seeping from a gash on his head on to and across the floury white stone floor.

'Look at me,' said Nehemiah, 'you could say I've come to bring you peace.'

'What?' Jonathan asked, confused.

'What peace?' Nehemiah smiled, 'that's a good question. Why, it's the peace, I suppose, that comes with oblivion.' Still calm and soft–voiced, he laid down the musket, drew out the knife and stepped forward. Jonathan, frozen, could only stare at him. Nehemiah slashed open Jonathan's shirt, ripping the surface of the flesh beneath. Blood spread slowly out, making a jagged line of red against the boy's pale skin.

*　*　*

Wayland slowed instinctively as he approached the bakery. Trying hard to concentrate, he tried to filter out the hullabaloo of shouting, crashing and shrieking in the town and to focus on the building before him. He thought he heard a low murmur and breathed out with relief. If that was Alun talking it was likely with Jonathan. He lowered his weapon and quietly pushed open the door. In an instant Wayland took in the scene before him: Alun bleeding on the floor, a man cutting at Jonathan. He leapt at the man, catching him a sideways blow on the shoulder and pushing him away. Jonathan stood as if frozen, the red line widening across his pale chest. 'Get down!' Wayland yelled at his son.

But Nehemiah was quicker. In one move he'd seized Jonathan and flung the boy's body in front of himself. His knife was now at Jonathan's throat.

Wayland paused. 'Who in Hell are you?' he asked Nehemiah, 'He's a just a boy. He took no part in this accursed war. What can he be to you?'

'Ah, the father,' Nehemiah said, 'and also then the husband. Or rather, a man who was a husband.'

Wayland noticed then the man's jagged half ear just as Jonathan spoke. 'Father, he... he's the one. The one who killed –'

A blow from the hilt of Nehemiah's knife silenced Jonathan. His head lolled to one side, but Nehemiah still held him firmly by the neck, his knife at the ready.

'Who?' Wayland began. But even as he said it realisation began to course, forcing its way through his head and through – it felt – his very veins. He knew, without knowing exactly how he knew, that Rebecca's killer was standing before him. The intense lust for revenge that he'd nursed for so long took over, the lust of his nightmares, the same lust that had ruled so many of his waking hours.

A fog of red swirled in front of his eyes and he gripped hard on the branding iron.

'I know what you're thinking. But you'll not do it. For I have your boy.' Nehemiah's words cut through the fog somehow and Wayland found his eyes focused on Jonathan's neck. He noted the knife, he looked into Nehemiah's eyes and he saw the man's utter determination. He stood, stock–still. The branding iron was still behind him, still in his left hand.

'Don't you want to know?' Nehemiah asked.

'Know what? What is it you want?'

'Know how she died. Your wife. The plump little whore.'

Wayland said nothing.

'She did call out for you, you know,' said Nehemiah, 'but of course you weren't there.'

A noise – it was half grunt, half sob – escaped from Wayland. Nehemiah tightened his grip on the knife and two more crooked lines of blood appeared, this time on Jonathan's neck, above and below the knife's edge.

Wayland felt paralysed as shock and horror hit him. He saw Jonathan's neck move very slightly, his muscles stiffening, and he guessed then that the boy was conscious.

'She survived the water trial, you see,' Nehemiah continued, 'but I knew she was a whore. They're all whores, you know. They all deserve it.'

Wayland stood rigid, his mind whirling but beginning to function, to calculate. His eyes caught a tiny movement behind Nehemiah. Could Alun too be conscious now? Wayland willed with all his might that this knowledge would not show in his face. 'So, you killed her?' he asked, playing for time now, 'That's all you're capable of is it? Killing defenceless women?'

Just then there was a crackle as some cinders toppled down in the bread oven furnace, provoking a small flare-up. Alun's eyes were swiveling around. Wayland prayed he was taking in the situation.

'I did,' said Nehemiah, 'but you're wrong. They're not all defenceless. Usually I enjoy a bit of fight back first.'

'All?' asked Wayland. He was stalling again, just trying to keep the man talking while he thought for a way to get at Nehemiah. He gripped the branding iron tighter. It was still out of Nehemiah's range of vision. He saw Alun silently coiling one leg up. Wayland shouted to distract Nehemiah.

'Why? In God's name, why?' He was yelling now at Nehemiah and he took a step forward to distract him further.

Then it all happened in an instant. Alun lashed out with his foot, catching Nehemiah at the back of knee, bringing that side of the man down. Jonathan hit out with his fist, straight up and through Nehemiah's arm. And Wayland caught Nehemiah a blow on the shoulder with the branding iron. The knife fell to the floor and Jonathan, bleeding heavily from the arm he'd hit out with, was free. Alun, though, passed out again from the pain of his exertion.

39.

ayland had Nehemiah now, pinned to the wall. He glanced at Jonathan, decided he'd live and turned his attention back to Nehemiah. Now that the man was no longer armed he seemed to deflate completely. Wayland realised to his surprise that his captive had little resistance in his arms. But this was only the briefest of his thoughts. Much more intense were his thoughts of revenge. Pent up for so long, they crowded back into Wayland's mind now and he forgot everything else – the breaking of the siege, Alun, even Jonathan. He was totally focused on the one thing. He raised up the branding iron he'd brought with him and held it over his prisoner's head. He was tempted, very tempted, to smash it down, to beat out the man's brains in one go. Flashes of his dream of vengeance came back to him. He realised that would be too quick. He wanted something more. It was second nature for him to think in terms of fire, of burning flesh, as he had before, with Carter. Easily holding Nehemiah against the wall with his right hand, he reached out with his left to open the bakery's oven door. The fire inside was low but a healthy red colour. He thrust the branding iron into the furnace and held it there, counting silently as he was wont to do in the smithy when heating up horseshoes to shape them.

As soon as Wayland judged it to be ready, he pulled the iron back from the fire. He took care to pause so that Nehemiah too could admire its glowing aura. Wayland could feel its heat on his face. His nose took up the familiar smell of molten iron. He drew in his breath and spat on the iron's end just to hear the hiss of steam. Nehemiah shrank back into the wall as far as he could. He opened his mouth to speak or scream but not a sound came out. Wayland brought the iron slowly closer and closer. He held it to the man's cheek and watched it melt the flesh. Nehemiah screamed now, a high-pitched long and gurgling wail. Wayland held the iron steady.

'Man, what are you doing? Stop, stop for the love of God, he's still one of Fairfax's men – they'll kill *us*.' Alun's voice finally cut through to Wayland's consciousness. He dropped the iron to the floor. With both hands, he pulled Nehemiah to the centre of the bakery. 'Happen I should cool the poor man down, then.' he said. There was a harsh edge to his voice, one that Alun had never heard before.

The bakery had a large sink. The water in it was dark but clear. Wayland seized Nehemiah by his long, lank hair, marched him across to the sink and plunged him face down into the water, pushing his head down until it hit bottom. Then he pulled him up again and shook the head, as a dog shakes a rat. He wrenched him up bodily, jerking the man's face round roughly to face him. Nehemiah heaved and coughed. Water poured off him, dirty white globules of bread flour clung to his face.

'Wait.' the man gasped. 'Not water. I will tell you anything.'

'And why not water? I doubt you cared one jot when my Rebecca begged against the water.'

'I killed them, it's true.'

'You go for the weak, the vulnerable. What sort of pathetic man are you?'

'No…'

'No what?'

'No, not the weak. The unguarded. I like…' Nehemiah's face twisted into a sneer. He had lost some of his fear. 'You asked so I'll say it,' he continued, 'I need to take time. I like them with a bit of fight. At the beginning. So that I can see them change. See them realize their guilt.'

'Guilt? What guilt?' Wayland, beside himself, was spluttering now. It seemed to him that Nehemiah was switching between two forms like a shape shifter: one a cowardly wretch and the other an arrogant bully.

'Whoredom. Bitch dogs with lust.' he said, the bully in him in the ascendant again.

Wayland cracked him across the face with his fist. The change was instant.

'Stop, don't. Maybe like you say your wife was innocent but…'

'Maybe? What do you mean maybe? And innocent of what?' asked Wayland.

'The others, they were whores. The Bible…'

'I've no time for your bible reading or your warped morality. And that poor boy? The one you mutilated? Was that just before you crossed my path back then? What was it in that mixed up hell of your mind that *he* was guilty of?'

With each word Wayland shook Nehemiah until his teeth rattled and a gurgling sound came from his throat.

'I, I thought,' he stammered, 'I thought he was a witness, your boy that saw…'

Wayland realised then that Nehemiah must have been hoping to kill Jonathan when he killed the boy. And he, Wayland, had allowed this man into his home. He stared at Nehemiah, speechless. He found that somehow the heat of his fury had drained away, but a steely calm had filled its place instead. Slowly but steadily he pushed Nehemiah down into the sink again. He held on longer this time and lifted him only little by little.

'We can't, we can't *kill* him, Father, we can't do that.' Jonathan's voice was weak but his distress was clear.

Wayland paused but he didn't turn round. As the water stilled though, its floury suds now gone, Wayland suddenly saw himself, clearly mirrored, in the sink. His face was distorted – horribly so – with hate. Still holding Nehemiah's hair, he froze. He didn't like what he saw. Only a minute ago, all he could think of was killing. He had lusted for it these twelve months past – and, he knew, he had wholly relished breathing in this man's fear. Now, a slow numb horror came over him. What had he become, to carry out such a killing in front of his son? And at what risk would it be to the boy if they must answer to Fairfax for such a death?

Wayland's arms dropped slowly. Nehemiah shuffled away. There was a pungent smell of urine and a yellowy trail began to puddle behind him. There was a groan from Alun and Wayland saw that he was conscious again, opening his mouth only to shut it again. Wayland thought though that he seemed to be agreeing with Jonathan.

'No, lad, I… I suppose we should not.'

'I thought… I thought you were going to kill him.'

Wayland flushed darkly and stared down at the stone floor. Minutes passed. 'It is a shame we can't, though,' he said finally, his mood stabilising. He looked at Nehemiah. 'You!' he spat, 'All this time I've thought of you, not knowing you. I saw you as some kind of evil monster, a massive, threatening force. But now I see you quite properly. You're sick. You're some kind of a perversion of a being. But most of all, you are a pathetic shadow of a man. You're not even worth the effort of killing.'

The others turned too, to look at Nehemiah. With his skinny body seeming to droop, snot dripping from his nose and the wet patch spreading across his breeches he did indeed look wretched. The searing from the iron had left a clear and vivid brand on his face, alongside his nose. Wayland realized that it was Sir Charles Lucas's own branding iron that he had used. He must have wielded it at an angle though, for the "L" had come out more like a "V".

'For all to see,' said Alun, 'now you have the V. The V for the villain that you are.'

Wayland thought a moment. 'And V for vengeance,' he said, 'my vengeance. At last. And for as long as you may live.'

Nehemiah stared at them; he was only slowly beginning to comprehend as he felt his cheek and his fingers carefully traced the letter there. The depth of the mark told him it really would be permanent. He turned to leave – and then he fled. Jonathan called out after him. 'People will see that V and they will think Vagrant,' he said, 'you'll be chased out from every place, be it village –' he stressed the V in "village" '– or town.' He laughed, a harsh laugh, but a laugh nevertheless.

Nehemiah stumbled as he ran. They watched him stagger along the street.

'You'll never outrun that mark!' Jonathan called out after him.

Wayland turned his attention to the injuries of his companions. He took an old jerkin Alun had left slung over a table, tore it quickly into strips and bandaged their wounds. Alun's head wound looked the most serious injury, but the bleeding had slowed and Wayland remembered how head wounds sometimes produced more blood than lasting injury. He saw with relief that Jonathan's injuries were only superficial, but he didn't feel any better about them until he had them covered over. He'd barely finished his administrations when he realized that the hullabaloo of the invading chaos was getting louder, nearer to the bakery.

40.

*E*vents moved swiftly over the next twenty–four hours. Fairfax's officers soon began asserting order and control over their troops. All the besieged men in Colchester were rounded up, separated from the women and then further divided according to whether they were civilian or military. Both Jonathan and Alun were readily acknowledged by Fairfax's men to be civilians – Jonathan because of his age and Alun, initially because of his appearance though the clinching factor was his throaty cough and floury phlegm, the clear signs of baker's lungs. Wayland they suspected at first, until he showed them his smithy tools and explained the circumstances of his forced labour for the King's side.

The morning after the siege had broken began very differently from the mornings of the previous eleven weeks. The most noticeable difference was the lack of sound.

There was no firing, no bombardment or restoration of the ramparts, just the purposeful hum of orders being passed on and carried out. Wayland soon learnt that the King's foot soldiers had been ordered to pile up their weapons and to line themselves up near the East Gate. The few surviving horses were to be gathered up and taken to St Mary's churchyard, together with all the saddles and bridles. Since there was, of course, a great imbalance in these numbers a small party had been ordered to assist in transporting the tack that had belonged to the many now dead horses. One of Fairfax's men ordered Wayland to help in this. Wayland guessed there were only a little over a hundred horses left alive. They were all cavalry horses; not a single civilian horse had escaped the terrible hunger of the town's civilian population. Wayland reflected that at least his own horses had not suffered that fate. These surviving horses made a pathetic picture: their heads hung down, ribs thrusting out, the girths hanging loose under their saddles. It took Wayland and the other men many trips to take so many now redundant saddles over to the collection point and like most of his group, Wayland quickly felt feeble from so much effort after the privations of the siege. Finally, though, it was done and even the Parliamentary soldier overseeing the task looked relieved.

Wayland had hoped that they would be free to return home straightaway but it soon became clear that lengthy discussions were under way concerning the separate fates of the King's officers and commanders and the King's lower ranking men. Until these discussions were concluded there would be little opportunity for him to press their own case. Royalist tactics and in particular their refusals of Fairfax's earlier terms of surrender had effectively left both men and officers totally at the mercy of the Parliamentary side – and Fairfax's blood was up. Rumours of imminent summary executions abounded. Meanwhile, the main preoccupation of the townspeople, over and about resisting any further looting, was of course for food. A train of mules, laden with foodstuffs, followed surprisingly quickly after the siege's end and everyone who could get near enough was final able to eat. Wayland cautioned his little group, including now Alice, against eating too much at first.

Wayland's next step was to seek some more lasting treatment for the wounds on both Jonathan and Alun. At Alice's own suggestion she approached the women in the Parliamentary camp who had charge of bandages and the like for their men. She traded some of her remaining store of woven cloth for a small supply of ointments and some clean-looking bandages. As soon as she had changed their dressings they discussed together how best to raise with their new masters the question of leaving Colchester. The town's original blacksmith had reappeared, and Wayland thought it politic to leave the smithy to him, so they crowded round in the bakery. Rowland was busy there, firing up his furnace and pounding the new supplies of flour into a great mixing sink. Wayland's first suggestion was that as the man less likely to be of any interest or use to the army Alun should be the one to seek official permission at the earliest opportunity for himself and Wayland to leave Colchester and return home to their own part of the county. Then Alice spoke. She said she was fearful that trade in Colchester, more specifically the wool trade which had, anyway, provided her with only a tenuous livelihood before the siege, would take a while to pick up again – if it ever did. With her home damaged and looted of most of its few contents, she had little else to keep her in the town. Wayland considered whether his blacksmithing back in the village could sustain all three of them – if only they could return there. And if she would want to join him. He thought it might. So he made her the offer of a home. Alice looked first to Wayland and then to Jonathan. The boy smiled his approval and she accepted, knowing that they would live as man and wife, whether married in church or not. They agreed that if they could secure a permit to leave the three of them should travel closely together. Wayland and Alice kissed on the deal. Alun let out a low, lewd whistle.

Alice tried to pull Jonathan into a three–way embrace but both Wayland and the boy shrugged her arms away.

'Love birds! Disgusting, don't you reckon?' Rowland muttered, catching Alun's eye. 'I'll be well rid of the lot of you. So much so that I have a plan to help you.'

'You do? But what influence can you have? You're just a baker. I cannot but doubt you have connections.' Wayland, disbelieving and slumped on a stool, was fast becoming despondent after the rush of so many emotions and realizing his new responsibilities. Alun, however, was beginning to recover his usual buoyant mood. 'Just a baker? Did I hear you aright? And I thought we had the relationship friends have. Some respect, please!'

'Come,' Rowland said to Alun, indicating the street with a nod of his head, 'let us leave this man – this just a smith – and see what we lowly bakers can achieve.'

Some two hours passed. For Wayland and Alice these were long and mostly silent hours. They could hear a distant buzz from the street as gossip and rumour circulated concerning the fate of Lucas and his fellow commanders. Wayland wasn't interested in them. His own view was that Lucas had judged matters badly with his persistent and unrealistic expectations of reinforcements and he regarded the man with the weary annoyance a servant has for a master whose nature steers him to mistake. Most of all, Wayland simply wished himself home. At last Alun returned, alone but triumphant. He waved at Wayland with four passes to leave Colchester in his hand.

'They have the seals of authority an' all,' he said, 'but I'm not about to share with you, a mere smith, the secret of my success. However, you shall have the headache of determining how we shall travel home, with no horses.'

Wayland didn't trouble himself to reply but he had of course been thinking about that. He began now a quick assessment of the few assets they still had between them. He himself possessed some money left from the brief period very early on during the siege when Lucas had ordered for him to be paid for his blacksmithing duties. Money had lost its value in the town, of course, during the past few weeks but its recovery on the siege's ending was instant. He doubted though that it was enough to buy three horses, but he set out to enquire anyway. There were none to be bought nearby. So next he checked their footwear and asked Alice if she would be able to manage a few rough repairs to their boots where needed. As soon as she had done that, they set off, on foot, trusting to God or Fortune to help them. While they were relieved to leave the town at last they were all were somewhat daunted at the thought of such a long walk. Still, as Wayland reminded them, the King's infantry had managed a much longer walk in the other direction to reach Colchester.

As they trudged along the road south, they passed first a long, straggly line of prisoners. They recognized a few of the King's foot soldiers. Most of them had been partly stripped; many were bruised or worse. All of them held their heads down as they shuffled along roped together. In sharp contrast their captors and guards, the lower ranks of Fairfax's "model" army, laughed and joked, aiming a kick at their captives whenever they ran out of conversation.

'Where will they be taking them, Father?' Jonathan asked.

'I heard some talk that they're being sent to the place they talk of as the New World,' Wayland replied, 'they'll be set to work there for some period. Then they will be allowed to return.'

'Not that I've ever heard of one who did return,' Alun commented, 'and not that I care especially what becomes of them.'

'But...' Jonathan said, a frown creasing his forehead, 'I thought the terms of surrender said to allow them to return home?'

Wayland thought for a moment. 'The thing is, I think, son, that those in command often find a way to vary matters – and always they do so in their own favour. You'll probably find they'll say later that they did not hear these men swear not to bear arms against the Parliament ever again. Or maybe they have judged them guilty of some other crime than soldiering: theft, treachery or the like.'

'Or being poor,' added Alun.

'Being poor? But how can that count as a crime?' Jonathan asked, puzzled.

Wayland looked at Alun, hoping he would come up with an answer. Just then, however, Jonathan reached over and grabbed Wayland's arm. 'Look,' he said, 'look who it is.'

It was Nehemiah. Unlike the others, he was attached to a burly soldier by a chain rather than a rope.

'But he was one of Fairfax's own men, wasn't he?' Jonathan whispered.

Alun signaled to him to wait until they were well past Nehemiah. 'I reckon I know what did it,' he said, 'it was the 'V' you branded him with. I said it would serve him ill. Likely Fairfax's men took more notice of that than the man's own rantings of innocence.'

Wayland thought about that. He was surprised to discover that it nether neither angered nor pleased him. He just didn't care. He did think, though, that Fate had granted some small token of justice there: the symmetry of the brand mark that ran along Nehemiah's nose, like the slashes on the women of Naseby. Alun, walking alongside him, seemed to guess his thoughts for he looked at Wayland. 'A child murderer,' he said, 'I for one would wish him some worse death.'

They were some yards away, past Nehemiah when they heard shouting. Wayland turned round in time to see Nehemiah make a break for it. He must have overpowered his guard and ripped the chain's end from him because now he was lashing the poor man round the head with it. Wayland guessed he'd used the element of surprise coming from one of his sudden mood shifts, from defeated felon to determined murderer. Nehemiah then ran off, toward the London road, zigzagging his way. Fairfax's men shouted after him but only one man was quick enough to take up his musket and fire. That one musket ball was sufficient. It dropped Nehemiah to the ground. His body shuddered once and then was still.

'I told you vengeance belongs to God,' Alun said. Wayland said nothing but he did think to himself that perhaps it would be fairer to acknowledge that he had helped the Lord some in that venture.

41.

In fairness, Fairfax's thirst for revenge had only begun far more recently than Wayland's. It was – or so he told himself – not so much an emotion but the logical and balanced response to the events of the siege. He wanted to believe himself free of passion and all other unruly feelings. He pursued it, however, with just as much stubborn determination as Wayland had devoted to his own pursuit of revenge. The way Fairfax saw things, the King's commanders in Colchester were traitors who had in addition caused the brutal and needless suffering of the town's citizens by causing the siege to drag on for so long. The losses on his own side – well over five hundred of Parliament's besieging army had been killed or died during the siege – added considerably to his sense of grievance. As an experienced military commander he expected to lose men in battle. That's what happened in war. It was to be accepted. But this siege should not have taken the path it did, with so much pointless fighting. So now it was largely down to him to take the winning side's decisions. Thinking it through, considering what retribution to take and how to take it, Fairfax knew that the Lords Capel, Loughborough and Norwich were beyond his reach: he could advise but only Parliament itself could rule on the fates of men of such elevated rank. But that was all right. He knew too that Lucas – and to an extent, albeit lesser, Lisle – had in practice been the real strategists behind the key decisions anyway. And he should have a free hand in deciding their fate. He would need to follow the correct procedure though. Quickly, he set up a council of war in lieu of a military court. This body would be charged with deciding forthwith the fate of four of his key prisoners: Sir Charles Lucas, Sir George Lisle, Colonel Farre and Sir Bernard Gascoigne. They had surrendered, as he'd ordered, and were currently held in the town's chief inn except, that is, for Farre who was reported to be hiding out somewhere. Fairfax liked the irony of this inn's name. He hoped his captives would feel it too, less comfortably. The inn's name was The King's Head. The charge, he announced, was to be no less than that of High Treason.

That the penalty for High Treason was severe was a fact well known by all, throughout England. Within living memory, the so-called Gunpowder Plot had led to the death and sustained mutilation of its chief plotter. Since then, though, Parliament had decreed an official end to torture because Parliament of course regarded itself as so much more merciful than the King's regime had ever been. Fairfax, too, liked to regard himself as a humane man, even a progressive one. Besides, these traitors were knights of the realm, not rabid Catholic spies. A firing squad, then, clean, efficient and quick, would be both appropriate and sufficient. He decided though that he would not, at this stage, inform his prisoners about any aspects of punishment. Let them stew in doubt, fear and the cruel delusion of hope.

As Fairfax had expected, discussion on the case in the council of war was short. One of his generals did advocate a more lenient approach. Another, General Ireton, spoke vehemently in favour of a death penalty. Fairfax made a show of hesitation, hoping to appear undecided. He soon gave up any pretence, though, that he could actually come down on the side of mercy. The verdict went his way, but its implementation suffered a couple of setbacks. Farre was still missing and Fairfax was further thwarted in his pursuit of revenge by the discovery that a second prisoner, Sir Bernard Gascoigne, was Italian and so must not be executed for fear of upsetting a foreign power. As soon as the decision in favour of the death penalty had been agreed, Fairfax summoned and sent off one of his colonels to the King's Head inn with orders to march the remaining two prisoners direct to the castle and from there, only a short time afterwards, to their place of execution.

42.

urther along the way, after Wayland's little party had finally finished passing the long straggling line of prisoners, they came to Fairfax's infantry, marching in a more orderly fashion in pairs though slowly, limited as they were to the pace of those carrying supplies. Wayland wondered idly if he might recognise any of his former fellow soldiers from the earlier war. Sure enough, he did see one: Jeb, a man with whom he had been billeted during a long wait outside some town in the west of the country. They had not really hit it off then. Jeb had liked playing pranks on his fellows and was talkative. Wayland of course was not. Wayland jerked his head away before they drew level and Jeb failed to notice him. Wayland scanned the long column ahead. His eyes picked out a kink in the line and he kept them focused on that as they very slowly progressed along the line. Alice was chatting away with Alun and Wayland felt more than a pang of envy at the easiness of their discourse. He looked back at the kink in the otherwise straight line of soldier and then over at Jonathan. The lad seemed to know immediately that his father had spotted something.

'What is it Father?' he asked. Then he too saw the irregular bulge ahead. His young eyes were keener than Wayland's. 'It's a horse,' he said, 'no, wait – it's two horses. No, it's four horses.'

They kept watching until they drew near. Jonathan realised it first. 'Father, it's them! Our horses!'

'You're imagining that, because you want it to be them,' Wayland replied, but he saw that the profiles of the horses were familiar and he found himself doubting his own words even as he said them. By the time they were some fifty steps away there could be no doubt that the middle two horses were theirs. Wayland immediately thought of the danger of the situation. Jonathan would want to claim the horses. Any hint of an accusation of theft could result in real trouble for all of them and anyway there was certain to be some rule or law governing booty in times of war. He warned the boy not to say anything – though the irony of such a command struck him even as he worried about the situation.

They all watched keenly as they slowly advanced on the horses. As they approached, it became clear that the one lone soldier riding was having problems leading the other three horses. His own horse was dancing sideways and pulling at the bit with impatience. The other three horses were considerably thinner, lethargic and unwilling to walk on. The soldier jerked their ropes repeatedly, cursing them loudly each time.

Wayland fumbled through his pack of belongings. He turned to Alun.

'Have you any money? Any at all, any stash you've not mentioned?' he hissed.

'Why? What's up?' Alun asked but he delved into his breeches nevertheless and reached out several coins.

Alice looked at Wayland. She saw the intensity in his face. 'I have some,' she said, a little shame–faced, as she had not declared it earlier, 'I was saving it for… never mind, here, take it.'

Wayland looked at it. It was a surprisingly large amount. He hesitated. He looked over at Jonathan. The boy's face, shining with excitement, made up his mind. He reached for Alice's hand and he looked her straight in the eyes. 'I will pay you back,' he said, 'it may take time but I swear it.'

She nodded. 'I know.'

Wayland took a deep breath. This was going to be difficult. He sped up. He was about ten yards from the horses when there was a yell. 'Wayland! Is that you? What in God's name are you doing here? We heard you went back to your smithy – and a quiet life with the wife!' The shouted call came from a soldier nearby. The man broke ranks, came up to Wayland and slapped him on the back.

Wayland winced at the mention of his wife but quickly adjusted his expression, recognising the man and realising that this could maybe work to his advantage. 'Edmund! Long time since I set eyes on you. I've been trapped in that accursed town. More than half–starved we were.'

'There's always room for one more in the model army – if you're tempted. I can put in a word for you. Always willing to help an old comrade,' the soldier replied with a broad smile.

'I think not,' said Wayland, 'but tell me, what do you know of those horses?'

'Them? Oh, yes, that was strange enough. Taz – or Dutchie, as we call him – found them wandering about near our trench. To be truthful with you, he's not a great horseman and he doesn't know how to handle them or what to do with them. But he's damned if he'll let them go again. Thinks he can sell them.'

'See, the thing is,' Wayland said, 'the thing is, that two of them look like the two we lost during the siege. And, well, whether they are or no, I'd like to buy them.'

'I'll tell you what. I'll put in a word for you, introduce you, like. Don't worry about the Dutch thing. He speaks English well enough now.' He pushed his way forward and Wayland fidgeted as he watched the two men talk. Then he noticed that his old horse was saddled with his saddle – and the saddlebag was still attached. He went over to the three horses. Brownie, his own horse, snickered with recognition. Edmund had clearly explained matters to Taz. The Dutchman looked interested. 'To tell the truth, these horses are becoming a big pain,' he said, 'being as they are so thin and poor. But my orders, see, are to bring them whether they will or no. The army needs to make up for losses in the siege and it may be some needy soul might buy them when we reach town.'

Wayland looked back at Edmund. From the way Edmund winked at him, Wayland figured that the "orders" were likely no more than a ruse to up the price.

'Happen I could help you with that,' Wayland said, 'buy 'em now, sooner rather than later.'

Taz looked unconvinced.

'What would you take for those two?' Wayland asked, pointing out his two.

'No.' replied Taz.

'No? But you have to sell them anyway.'

'One stupid horse is as bad and near as much work as three stupid horses,' Taz said, spitting into the dirt.

Wayland, realising what the man wanted, sighed. 'Oh, all right then,' he said, 'how much would you take for the three?'

They bartered a while. Wayland had to remind Taz how far away the next big town was and how much work towing the three would likely be. He pointed to the man's hands, already chafed raw from pulling on the ropes. But Taz was a man who knew a keen buyer when he saw one. He named a price he said was a final figure. Wayland's money, taken with that from both Alun and Alice fell short of the amount. Wayland went to undo his pack of belongings. He pulled out a couple of blacksmithing tools and showed them to the man. 'Well,' said Taz, 'I suppose they might sell or come in useful.'

Taz pulled Edmund aside and they whispered a while. As far as Wayland could tell, Taz was seeking assurances from Edmund that in selling to Wayland he would run no risk of being accused of assisting an enemy by selling him horses. He came back to Wayland. 'Done.' he said. Just then, they noticed in the distance what looked like an officer on horseback coming in their direction. Money, tools and horses changed hands in an instant and Wayland muttered his hurried thanks to Edmund. He led the horses away, over to the others. Jonathan of course was overjoyed. He scrambled up on to Runaway Tom, bareback. Wayland ran his hand down the legs of all three horses. Satisfied there were no injuries, he went to lift Alice on to Brownie. There was some flouncing of skirt and petticoat as she struggled to sit aside the horse. It was her first time on horseback and Wayland had to show her how to hold the reins and grab on to the saddle if need be. 'I know it's not ladylike,' he said with a grin, 'but what I am sure of is that it beats walking.'

'That it does, for certain,' said Alun, 'and you can tell that boy I'll be looking to have my turn on the old runaway before too many miles.'

The third horse was so thin and scraggy he didn't dare put a rider on its back. As they parted way from the army, the little group felt that things were finally looking up. Hope, though, was tinged with more than a little apprehension as they thought of the long journey ahead. Wayland wondered just what they would find on their return.

$\mathcal{43}.$

If Fairfax had thought about it at all beforehand, he would have expected the completion of his revenge by means of the executions of Lisle and Lucas to give him some satisfaction. He did conceive of the deed as sending a clear signal to all, Royalists and Parliamentarians alike, that the betrayal of one's word represented treason and deserved the highest penalty. What he could not possibly have foreseen, however, was that by their brave and outspoken approaches to death both Lucas and Lisle would achieve a kind of immortality, one that fired the people's imagination and sent a very different message: one of courage and heroism. That message was to spread far beyond Colchester and Essex.

Sir Charles Lucas made a poignant speech before his executioners. First, he justified all his actions by reference to his loyalty to the King, a higher duty, as he saw it and the right way for his actions. He asked God to forgive the firing squad. He then stood tall, his face seemingly untroubled, ripped open his own doublet and challenged the firing squad with a roar: 'Now, rebels, do your worst!' The soldiers responded by discharging their muskets and he fell down dead.

By this time it was late in the day and darkening but the executioners would brook no delay. Sir George Lisle was brought forthwith to the same place of execution. Seeing the lifeless body of his fellow knight and friend Lucas before him, he knelt to kiss him before making his own impassioned justification of both his own actions and those of Lucas in resisting the siege. His generosity went one stage further than that shown by Lucas: he handed over a gold piece to the firing squad. He invited them to move closer whereupon one soldier replied, 'I'll warrant ye, sir, we'll hit you.'

Smiling, Lisle retorted 'I have been nearer you, friend, when you missed me,' before adding 'now then, rebels and traitors, do your worst.' His final words too were met with a hail of fire and his death.

Such obvious confidence and bravery on the part of both Lucas and Lisle in the face of death made a deep impression not only on those present but also on those who heard of it afterwards. And a great many people did hear of it, for ballads were rapidly composed, printed and widely distributed.

$$44.$$

The journey to Wayland's home territory was a long, hard slog but actually fairly uneventful. They reached Alun's village first, at about noon. Alun was riding on ahead, keen to be home again after all that had happened. The others hung back, with the intension of letting Alun be the first to greet his wife. As they approached his house, though, Alun raised his right arm, a silent signal to the others to stop. They pulled up the horses and listened. Alun walked back towards them.

'I can hear talking,' he hissed, 'and it sounds like it might be a man. Though I'm not sure.' His face was drained of all colour as his mind whirred with possible reasons for some man to be in his house.

They noticed then that there was a pony tied to a post by the cottage door.

'I'll go first,' said Wayland, 'see what's up. You stay with Alice and the boy.'

He dismounted, handing over his reins to Jonathan and strode firmly but silently up to the door. He did knock but he opened the door at the same time. Rosie May, Alun's wife, called out straightaway. 'Wayland! You're back.' She flung her arms round him, much to his surprise. He looked round the room, but he could see no sign of any man.

'And Alun?' she asked, 'Where is he... or has he...' Her hand flew to her mouth. 'Tell me!'

Wayland went to the window to wave Alun over, but he hesitated. He lowered his voice. 'Do you not have company? I heard a man's voice.'

'What? Oh, that's just Rees,' she said. She saw his bewilderment. 'He's grown. His voice has changed as boys' voices do.'

'Rees? Thank God but how...' he stopped, realising that of course Rosie May was still desperate for news of her husband. This time he did beckon at the door and Alun, Alice and Jonathan came over, leaving their horses tethered to the railing outside the cottage. Alun embraced his wife but his stiff arms told Wayland that he was still unsure.

'You must tell all about it, how you're here, what kept you...' her words came out in a rush until she saw how stunned Alun still was. 'I'll get some beers.' said Rosie May, pulling out jugs, 'Boy, come see.'

'Boy?' Alun muttered.

A tall but skinny youth walked into the kitchen and stood awkwardly. 'Rees came by a week ago,' Rosie May told them, 'he brought news,' she put her hand on Alun's arm. 'I'm sorry, love, but Agnes is dead and...'

'I know,' said Alun, 'at least, that is, I believed so. But how does he know? And come to that, where has he been these past years?'

'My mam and... and that man she was with after she left my father, well they took me everywhere with them. We – Mam and I – we followed the army all over. It was difficult but sometimes it was exciting. Until that last battle, the one at Naseby it was,' said Rees, turning to face Alun. 'Mam looked out for me and as much as I could, I looked out for her. But it wasn't enough... I was only twelve then... and when the King's side was defeated and we knew that Fairfax's army was coming, well, she told me to go.' Tears fell down his face. 'And so, so... well, so I did. She said they would kill me. She thought she would be all right, being a woman and all. She was ready and willing to help with the wounded regardless of which side they fought on. She saw it as her duty – she was very strong about that.'

'If you were at Naseby,' Wayland asked, 'that says it all. We understand. We have heard it from others. You need not say it. And from what we've been told, no–one could have stopped the blood–letting.'

They sat down and Alun explained who Alice was and he started to tell his wife something – though not by any means everything – of the siege of Colchester, Nehemiah, and the aftermath of the Royalist surrender. They drank a few more beers with some bread and mutton. Rosie May started to bring them up to date with the village news, but she could tell it was not the right time for that. Wayland asked about his own village and was reassured to learn that as far as she knew, his smithy was still standing. The beer, the bread and the warmth in Alun's kitchen combined to set him into a contented reverie. While the others talked on, animated, Wayland thought about the runaway horse. Knowing it had been Nehemiah's horse explained a lot about its nervous and flighty behavior and its need to bond with Jonathan. He wanted to keep the horse but knew the men who had found the horse had some rights to claim the horse, according to custom. He reasoned, though, that maybe they would accept the third horse, maybe with a small payment, instead. What he had to figure out now was how to put enough money aside for that. If work picked up when he got his blacksmithing trade running again, he would probably soon have most of what would be needed. Jonathan was of an age now where he could be useful with a horse. He could bring in some money taking messages and the like to nearby villages.

Wayland finally began to feel some hope for the future – and hope was something that had been in very short supply for a very long time. His mind was brought back to the present day then by the sound of the door closing as Jonathan took Rees out to show him the horse. 'Husband,' he heard Rosie May say to Alun, 'about the lad, Rees. He has no family, with your sister having passed and by all accounts his father is nowhere to be found –' she spoke without pause – 'and, well, he's been useful this past week while you were away and I was stuck with the baking...'

Alun interrupted her. 'Don't fuss, wife. I think I know what you're leading up to,' he said, putting an arm around her, 'and yes, he can stay. So long as he knows he has to work. You know my lungs were always weak and the... well, the hard times in the siege have left me needing to recover my strength.'

Wayland knew that while Alun and Rosie May had a good marriage by many measures, it had always been a source of unhappiness to them that children had not followed. He wasn't surprised then when Rosie May flung her arms around Alun, thanking him again and again.

'Away with you, woman.' said Alun. He looked over at Wayland. Wayland knew it was time now to leave them. So he and Alice made their farewells with promises to meet up again soon and they set off with Jonathan. At first they rode in silence, as was their custom. Then Jonathan pointed to the horse he was riding. 'Father,' he asked, 'can we... is there any way we can...'

'Yes,' said Wayland, 'I reckon we can keep him. We'll fatten up this third one. Villagers should be happy with that one. If they can even remember the difference.'

'Yes!' Jonathan actually shouted. He turned to his father. 'We can't keep calling him Runaway Tom. Not after Fairfax and all that happened in Colchester. So, you see, I've been thinking what to call him...' he began – and he kept up his chatter all the way back to the smithy.

Author's Note

Some of the characters in this book actually existed and many of the events really did happen. Historians now agree that Matthew Hopkins, England's self-styled Witch-finder General, believed to have been responsible for the deaths of up to three hundred women between the years 1644 and 1646, died of consumption in Manningtree, Essex.

The bitter siege of Colchester occurred in the summer of 1648 when the English Civil War was reignited in several areas of Britain. It lasted eleven weeks and the besieged townspeople suffered horribly. To this day you can visit the spot where Lucas and Lisle were executed: the Lucas and Lisle Monument in Colchester Castle. Wayland and his story are however fiction and some of the words and deeds of actual historical figures have been fictionalised – but are not, I hope, out of character.

Bibliography/Further Reading

A true relation of that honourable, tho' unfortunate expedition of Kent, Essex, ad Colchester, in 1648. (A contemporary account by diarist Matthew Carter). Active 1660. 1750. Gale ECCO Print Editions.

The Notebooks of Nehemiah Wallington 1618 – 1654 A Selection. Edited by David Booy. Ashgate Publishing Limited. 2007.

The English Civil War Maurice Ashley 1990 Guild Publishing.

Understanding Popular Violence in the English Revolution: The Colchester Plunderers. John Walter. Cambridge University Press 2005.

Witchfinders: A Seventeenth–Century English Tragedy. Malcolm Gaskill. John Murray (Publishers). 2005.

The English Civil War 2000 Ed Peter Gaunt. Blackwell Publishers Ltd, Blackwell Essential Readings in History.

The Siege of Colchester, Phil Jones, 1648, 2003, Tempus Publishing Ltd.

The Siege of Colchester: Or An Event Of The Civil War, AD 1648 (1874), by the Rev. George Fyler Townsend, MA, Kessinger Publishing Legacy Reprint.

The Discovery of Witches: In Answer to severall QUERIES, LATELY Delivered to the Judges of Assize for the County of NORFOLK, by Matthew Hopkins, 1647.

Malleus Maleficarum: The Hammer of Witchcraft by Jacobus Sprenger and HeinrichKramer. The Folio Society. 1968.

Acknowledgements

My thanks to:

Professor Malcolm Gaskill because the detailed and vivid accounts in his book *Witchfinders: A Seventeenth-Century English Tragedy* first set me thinking about what was to become Wayland's story.

Matador for their expertise and patience in the publishing process for *Wayland's Revenge*.

Chris, Gerard, Michael and Catherine Hughes for some inspiration and assistance with digital technology.

Michael Hughes and Anne Coates for help checking drafts.

About the Author

*L*esley Lodge took her MA in Colchester. She worked as a journalist and then on regeneration projects and housing finance. She now lives on a smallholding in Bedfordshire, writing the next novel.

Her other publications include the Luton Literary Prize winning short story *Blues to Orange*, and *Joined Up Now,* another short story. She has also written a non-fiction book: *Lights! Camera! Gallop! The Story of the Horse in Film.*